# Wood Enders

## Trevor Roff

**Scripture Union**
130 City Road, London EC1V 2NJ

By the same author:
**New Boy at Wood End**

© Trevor Roff 1987
First published 1987

ISBN 0 86201 437 9

Phototypeset by Input Typesetting Ltd., London SW19 8DR
Printed by and bound in Great Britain by Cox and Wyman Ltd., Reading

# Contents

| | | |
|---|---|---|
| 1 | An accident – or was it? | 5 |
| 2 | Reactions | 15 |
| 3 | Relapse | 21 |
| 4 | Rusty | 31 |
| 5 | Ask for a miracle | 41 |
| 6 | Dancing and fighting | 51 |
| 7 | A surprise visit | 61 |
| 8 | Winners and losers | 69 |
| 9 | An invitation | 77 |
| 10 | A matter of life and death | 85 |
| 11 | Snooker, bikes and Jesus | 93 |

# 1

## An accident – or was it?

'Goodbye, Phil! And thanks for everything. It's been a smashing holiday!'

'It's been great to have you, Kevin. Just like old times! I wish you could have stayed longer.'

'So do I, but it's school next week. Holidays are over, whether we like it or not!'

'Yes, we're fourth years now. Senior pupils!'

'Look out! The train's moving. You'll have to get off!'

Kevin bundled his friend unceremoniously back on to the platform, then hung out of the window as the train gathered momentum. A sudden jolt separated the two out of talking distance and Kevin felt his stomach churn as his friend grew smaller.

'Keep in touch!' yelled a fast-receding Phil.

'You bet!' was the reply, but as Kevin waved his last farewell, he wondered whether he really meant it. Keeping up friendships across miles was not going to be easy, even when you'd been friends for over five years, as he and Phil had. As Kevin settled back into his corner seat for the two-hour journey to Liverpool Street, he reflected on his week's stay with Phil. It had been wonderful to wander round all their old haunts in and around Norwich, seeing old friends, enjoying old pastimes. For a while Kevin had felt he'd never been away. But as the week drew to an end, and the prospect of returning to his six-month old home in London loomed larger, there came with it a sense of finality. He was really saying goodbye this time to his old life, Norwich and Phil – not like last Christmas when things had been so rushed because of his dad's hurry to start his new job. Then he had never really left, not inside, and he'd always felt a stranger in his new school. This second departure had finally closed that part of his life, and Kevin instinctively felt it would be a long time before he saw Norwich again. The past was the past; he had a definite future now, one that he was determined to make the most of, as fourth year pupil at Wood End School.

The next Tuesday saw the great upheaval in hundreds of homes like Kevin's. Teenagers who had forgotten that seven am existed, found themselves staring at ringing alarm clocks or being rudely awakened by chiding parents. Kevin Chuck was no different; his carefree slumber shattered by his mother calling him into bleary-eyed wakefulness. Slowly he yawned himself into the day; then as full realisation came to him he jerked into life, ready to begin his first full year at Wood End. Two terms ago he had dreaded his first day; now he had a new start, new friends and a new purpose.

A few short months ago he had become a Christian, asking Jesus to sort out the mess he, Kevin, had made of his life. Now his past mistakes were behind him and he could face the future with confidence.

Kevin washed and dressed hurriedly so that he would have time to read his Bible and pray before breakfast. This was another part of his new life, which he'd never dreamed of last year. Now he didn't want to miss one day and resolved to make it an integral part of this new term.

The main gates of Wood End School saw a trickle of uniform-clad youngsters grow to a steady stream of pupils converging on the empty buildings and play-ground which had stood abandoned all summer, unchanged and unchanging, waiting for their return. On this first day, with most pupils obediently in uniform, the conformity of their outward appearance hid a bewil-dering assortment of emotions. The new first years ranged from nervousness to blind panic, while the other years felt both arrogantly superior to younger pupils and apprehensive at their own new situation.

Kevin joined the recognisable group of fourth years at one end of the playground. There were a few groups playing ball games but most preferred the anonymity of the large group. Kevin, too, sought out his friends.

'Ginger!' he called, as the unmistakable shock of red hair emerged into view.

'Hi, Kevin,' said Ginger. 'You look brown. Where have you been? The south of France?'

'No,' Kevin laughed. 'We couldn't afford a proper holiday this year, but I've just got back from Norwich. I got sunburnt from a day on the Norfolk Broads. But then I tan quite easily.'

'Lucky you. We couldn't get away either – Mum doesn't earn enough and I couldn't get a holiday job anywhere. All the casual jobs had gone, or men on the dole got them. It's been right boring this holiday. I'm glad to be back.'

'Yeh! Me too, in a way, though I'll probably feel different after a few lessons of maths. The place hasn't changed much, has it? Same old faces, too.'

'You're right. Hey! Look over there,' said Ginger, as a leather-jacketed individual came into view around the corner. 'Trust him to come dressed like that. On the first day too.'

The object of their attention was Gavin Daley, known as Gav to his mates, but called some less pleasant names behind his back by those who had experienced the rough treatment he and his gang meted out to those who got in their way. Kevin had good cause to remember meeting Gav on his first day at Wood End eight months ago, and he shuddered at the memory. Fortunately Gav had not noticed Kevin or Ginger and Kevin wondered if Gav still held a grudge against him for leaving his gang last Easter. He hoped that all of his first term here was well and truly in the past, and that Gav would let bygones be bygones.

His thoughts were interrupted by the loud ringing of the school handbell. Mr. Fletcher had made his appearance.

'Will all fourth years make their way to the Main Hall.'

With this sternly spoken instruction, the school year had begun. Mr. Fletcher, their Head of Year, was obviously starting as he intended to continue. Every pupil feared his wrath and made sure they kept on his good side, but otherwise few held any affection for him, as his moods and temper made him unpredictable and distant. 'Strange,' thought Kevin, 'he once terrified me. Now I feel rather sorry for him, doing a job he seems to hate.'

'See you later, Kev,' called Ginger as they were separated in the milling throng, pushing their way through the narrow doorway like salt in an egg-timer. He disappeared ahead just as Kevin felt an almighty thump from behind in his kidneys.

'Watch it! Who do you think you're pushing?' Kevin whirled on his assailant, then instantly regretted it. Staring right back at him with curling lip and sneering expression was Gav.

'I'm pushing you, Chuck. Any objections? Why don't you get out of the way like a good little boy and let the men go first?'

Kevin felt the anger welling up inside him at the deliberately mocking words and longed to be able to smash them back down Gavin Daley's throat, but he knew he was no match for the bullying gang leader. Gav saw the flicker of anger on Kevin's face and knew his remarks had hit home.

'Wanna make something of it, Chuck? I thought you religious goody-goodies believed in turning the other cheek.'. With a shout of laughter and another shove which knocked Kevin back into the throng, Gav elbowed

8

his way through the crowded doorway.

Kevin could feel his face burn with embarrassment as other fourth years saw that he had been made a fool of by Gav and had not stood up for himself. None of the others would have fought Gav either but it didn't stop some of them having their own dig at Kevin.

'Why don't you stick up for yourself, Kevin? You always were a bit of a weed,' said Lyn, an outspoken gum-chewing form-mate.

'What can you expect from one of the Jesus creeps?' said her friend Sarah. 'Do you still go to old Jenkins' Christian Union, then, Kevin?'

'Yes, I do,' said Kevin, finding his voice at last, and surprised at this sudden interest. 'Why don't you come along, sometime?'

'Ooh! Watch out, Sarah, he's trying to convert you!' laughed Lyn and the pair of them collapsed in a fit of giggles which only made Kevin even more the centre of attention. If only the ground would open up and swallow him!

Fortunately for Kevin, they were all kept busy for the next hour or so, writing out their new timetables and congratulating or commiserating with each other on their allotted teachers and subjects. Nevertheless, that small incident had left a dent in Kevin's self-confidence and his bright hopes for his fourth year were now edged with fear. He understood being afraid of Gav but he was surprised to realise that he was worried and nervous about what people like Lyn and Sarah thought of him.

The first Christian Union meeting of the term was not a happy one for Kevin. Last year he had grown to look forward to the weekly chatting, sharing and learning, and the cynical indifference of others had not bothered him. Today he felt more than ever conscious of people watching him and of what they might be saying behind his back, or even to his face, like Lyn and Sarah.

He entered Mr. Jenkins' room when he thought no-one was watching and made sure that he sat well away from the windows that overlooked the playground, in case curious idlers stared in. But even Mr. Jenkins' programme was against him; today they were improvising their own modern version of the Prodigal Son, ready for teaching on forgiveness next week. Everybody had to take part in one of the groups, and then to act it out in front of the others.

'Come on, Kevin, you as well, or this group will have a prodigal son without a father,' laughed Mr. Jenkins.

'Yes, come on Kev. Sally needs a husband in our group,' joked Darren, deepening Kevin's blush still redder.

So Kevin joined in, feeling rather a prune to begin with, until the infectious enthusiasm of the others finally warmed him to the task of welcoming home his junkie drop-out son.

Even so, as he confided to Ginger afterwards, he was dreading any other fourth years looking in and seeing him make a fool of himself.

'Yes, I know what you mean, Kev,' said Ginger. 'I wish sometimes that we could have the CU on the top floor where no-one could see us. But Mr. Jenkins did warn us last term that school is the toughest place to be a Christian, but that Jesus is pleased when we aren't afraid to stand up for him.'

'Yes, I know, but it's all right for you. You don't have Gavin Daley breathing down your neck. He's always poking fun at me every chance he gets. Really nasty too. I don't think he'll ever forgive me for leaving his gang.'

'It's not like you to be scared, Kev. Hey, don't you remember that time we had to take that watch back to Woolworth's? You were the one who stole it, but it was my knees that were shaking like jelly. You just walked straight into that manager's office and owned up to it as cool as a cucumber. You certainly weren't afraid then. I don't know how you did it.'

'That was just after I'd become a Christian, wasn't it?' said Kevin. 'I think I just felt so happy that Jesus had forgiven me it never occurred to me that the manager wouldn't.'

'He certainly looked as if he'd had the shock of his life when you gave him the watch back,' Ginger laughed at the memory. 'I bet it was the first time any shoplifter had brought him back stolen goods. He didn't even tick you off.'

Kevin smiled ruefully. The incident certainly had its funny side, even though he was ashamed of the theft itself. Suddenly Gav the bully didn't seem such an insurmountable problem after all. He changed the subject.

'Are you still biking this Saturday?'

'You bet. Why don't you come round tonight and we can map out a route,' offered Ginger.

'Sure, if your mum won't mind,' said Kevin.

''Course not. She's glad we're going – offered to make up a packed lunch for both of us. But I said could I bring you back for tea afterwards instead.'

'Great,' said Kevin, then summed up both their feelings: 'It's going to be an ace day.'

Saturday morning dawned bright and clear, with a heavy dew which hinted at the approaching autumn, but promised fair weather for a fifty mile bike ride. Kevin needed no nagging to get him out of bed and he even surprised his parents with an early morning cup of tea.

'What's all this, then, Kevin?' said Mr. Chuck. 'Up with the lark this morning aren't you?'

'Oh, Alan! I told you last night! He's going off with Ginger for the day, on their bikes,' explained Mrs. Chuck.

'Oh yes, good. Are you taking your fishing rods, too?'

'No, Dad,' said Kevin, rather exasperated at Mr. Chuck's poor memory. 'Like I said to Mum, we're going out to Chelmsford, a long hike. We'll be cycling nearly all day.'

11

Kevin avoided further cross-examination and after a rushed breakfast and a hectic scramble for last-minute things he'd forgotten, he left the house. He called for Ginger and they were soon on their way. The traffic was fairly busy at first, but once they had cleared the shopping streets and got on to the A12, travelling was much easier. They planned to go as far as they could for the first couple of hours, then try a side road they'd found on the map and head for what had looked like a promising picnic site. One o'clock found them stretched out on a grassy slope overlooking Hummingfield Reservoir munching some well-earned sandwiches. The warm weather had given them a raging thirst, so they spent the early afternoon looking for a shop to replenish their drink supply. Having reached the outskirts of Chelmsford they turned for home and by five o'clock they were just re-entering their home area, happily tired and proud of their successful day's ride.

'Coming on home for tea, then, Kev?'

'If you're sure your mum doesn't mind.'

'I told you,' Ginger reassured him, 'she's got it all ready for us. She'd be disappointed if you didn't come.'

Mrs. Webb had prepared a slap-up mixed grill which they devoured in front of the TV. She had missed Ginger's company during the day but had busied herself catching up on the week's housework. Kevin knew she was divorced and didn't know what to expect when he saw her. But she was very welcoming and motherly to them, the sort of person you quickly felt comfortable with.

'Well, I can see you boys were ready for that,' she laughed, looking at their empty plates. 'I'm not surprised, after that journey. There's apple pie to follow.'

'Great!' said Ginger and Kevin together.

After the meal they sat back, satisfied and content, alternately watching television and telling Mrs. Webb of the day's exploits. It was nearly eight o'clock before Kevin realised.

'Heck! I'd better be going. Mum and Dad'll be worried.'

'Yes, you had,' agreed Mrs. Webb. 'But don't worry. I'll phone your parents and tell them you're on your way.'

'Thanks a lot.'

'Have you got your lights, Kev? It's getting dark,' said Ginger.

'No, I haven't. Still, I don't mind walking. I've had enough strenuous exercise for one day.'

Kevin little realised how much he would regret those words as he set off to walk the mile or so home. He was happily day-dreaming about the best Saturday he'd spent for a long time and didn't notice the small group of leather-clad youths from the far end of the street.

'Well, if it isn't the little weed, Chuck,' sneered Gav. 'Chuckweed we ought to call you,' and he laughed at his own little joke.

'Yeah. Out a bit late, aren't we, little boy?' Terry joined in the fun. 'Walking your bike home like a good little boy?'

Kevin looked round at the all-too-familiar leering faces – Gav, Tone, Terry and Paul. To think, he'd once been one of them, had enjoyed being part of their activities. While he inwardly shuddered, he put on a brave face.

'Very funny, I don't think. If you don't mind I'm in a hurry, so move out of the way,' he brazened.

'That's no way to talk to us, Chuck,' said Gav, giving Kevin a prod that forced him to step back. 'Think you can tell us what to do, do you, like you did before? Well, I've not finished with you. You can't just leave our gang and get away with it. I've been waiting a long time to get even with you, Chuck, and now I've finally got the chance. Come on, lads, let's do him.'

This was it, thought Kevin, the moment he'd been

dreading ever since the beginning of term. But strangely, as the fists and knees came flying in, he didn't feel as scared as he thought he would be. In all the pain, he just wished they'd stop and go away.

But what no-one had seen was the loose paving stone that Kevin was backing towards, away from the flailing limbs of his attackers. As he jumped backwards to avoid a well-aimed kick from Terry, Kevin's heel caught on the offending slab, Terry's kick found its mark and Kevin was flattened like a tenpin. He fell heavily, saw stars and lay still. The gang stopped dead, uncertain.

'Blimey!' yelled Tone. 'You've knocked him out, Terry.'

'Not my fault,' retorted the heavyweight. ''it 'is 'ead on the pavement, didn't 'e?'

'Come on lads, let's scarper,' Gav ordered. 'We've done what we needed to.'

'But will 'e be all right?' said Tone.

'Yeah! Stop worrying. Serve the so-and-so right. Come on.' And with that they bolted down the street away from their unconscious victim, with only Tone giving a few worried backward glances.

# 2

# Reactions

Kevin awoke to find himself staring at whiteness. Where was he? Slowly he dragged back to his semi-conscious mind the memory of the fight – the punches and kicks, the fall and the searing flash of light before total oblivion. But where was he now? His blurred brain could not work it out and he lapsed into an uneven doze.

The next thing he knew was being moved swiftly through the air. He raised his head in panic, but the pain was so great that he groaned and lay back. A rush of cold air spread over his face as he found himself plunged into darkness. Then a friendly voice spoke.

'Take it easy, son. We're at the hospital now. You're in good hands.' The kindly ambulance man guided Kevin's stretcher through the flapping plastic doors of the accident department and Kevin relaxed into the security of knowing his welfare was in safer hands than his own.

He was wheeled into a curtained cubicle where he was dimly aware of the comings and goings of white-coated figures, feeling him, examining him, asking him questions. Eventually his parents arrived and he managed a weak smile at them, familiar faces in a dream of antiseptic unreality. Soon he had drifted back into sleep, a real sleep this time.

He awoke next morning to an uncomfortable light shining from yet more white walls, but higher this time than the ambulance's. Looking around he saw sheets, a bed rail and more beds, the unmistakable furniture of a hospital ward.

'Ah! You're awake, love! Sister told me to come round and see if you were. I've to give you a wash – Doctor's coming round in half an hour.'

The dumpy, middle-aged woman in the green uniform proceeded to bed-bath him. So expertly did she work that Kevin had hardly regained his senses by the time she had finished. When she had left, he felt his head. It had been swathed in tight crepe bandages and for a moment Kevin panicked. But there was no point in that and he sank back on his pillow, waiting impatiently for someone to allay his fear. Yet he still missed the arrival of his next visitors until they had approached his bed.

'Hello, Kevin. How are you feeling, son?' It was his dad, showing an emotion rare in him. His mother hugged him, as mothers will.

'We were so worried about you, Kevin. When you didn't come home last night, we didn't know what to do,' fretted Mrs. Chuck. 'We phoned Mrs. Webb and she said you'd left an hour ago and we were just about to phone the police when the hospital rang. We came straight away, only to be told there was nothing we could do. I didn't sleep a wink all last night.'

'All right, Doreen, don't go on,' said Mr. Chuck. 'The boy's going to be all right. As soon as these stitches are healed he'll be as right as rain.'

'Is that what these bandages are for?' asked Kevin.

'Yes, son, just a precaution. You gave yourself a nasty bump on the head – you'll have a whopper of a headache for a couple of days. But you didn't crack your skull – the X-ray showed that. And the doctor says you can come home.'

So it was relieved parents and an unsteady Kevin who left the hospital and made the journey home. Both Mum and Dad did all they could to make Kevin comfortable. Mrs. Chuck fussed around propping him up on cushions and preparing his favourite meal while Mr. Chuck sat and chatted.

'We brought your bike home,' he said. 'Found it in the road still there where you'd fallen. No damage done

– not a mark on it. Surprising really, as you came a pearler and knocked yourself out. How did it happen?'

'But I thought you knew,' began Kevin, then broke off.

'Knew what, son?'

'It wasn't an accident, Dad. I was pushed.'

'What?' said Mr. Chuck, his face darkening.

'It was some boys from school. They saw me walking home and, well, I suppose they started hitting me.'

'What!' thundered Mr. Chuck again. 'They beat you up and left you lying in the road unconscious? We'll see about that. I'm going to phone the police. What are their names?'

'Oh, leave it, Dad. You'll only make me more trouble at school – and anyway they didn't knock me out. I fell backwards and hit my head.'

Mrs. Chuck had entered the room at the sound of Mr. Chuck's raised voice and joined in the conversation.

'But boys don't just bully anyone, Kevin. Why did they pick on you?'

'Oh, Mum! I don't know.' Kevin tried to avoid this embarrassing interrogation. 'I suppose it was because I used to belong to their gang.'

'Oh, it's that mob, is it?' said Mr. Chuck. 'I should have known. You were well out of that, I can tell you. Though I don't know why you had to go all religious at the same time. Are you sure that wasn't why they picked on you?'

'Whatever do you mean, Alan?'

'Well, people do funny things sometimes. Anyway, it's got to stop, but I can see what you mean, son. If we go to the police for a case of bullying, it could make things worse for you. But only if you promise me,' and Mr. Chuck emphasised his words, 'that you'll tell me if they ever try that again.'

'OK, Dad,' said Kevin. 'Can we have some lunch? I'm starving.'

17

The remark broke the tension and restored the family togetherness that Kevin's accident had created.

Kevin had time that afternoon to brood on his father's words. Why did Gav and the others hate him so much? Was it just because he'd deserted their gang? But others had formed passing friendships with bullies when it suited them, then broken them when they no longer felt threatened. Was it because he was religious, like Dad said? But surely God wouldn't let that happen? He was on God's side now. Surely God would protect him. God owed him that much at least.

As Kevin sat and brooded, his mood became blacker and angrier. Why hadn't God stopped the bullies? Did God really care what happened to him? Why didn't God look after him? After all, Kevin prayed to him every day and read his Bible. He'd done his bit, but God had let him down. Maybe he had displeased God in some way, maybe . . . maybe he wasn't a Christian after all? Those and a host of other similar thoughts bombarded Kevin, and his earlier happy mood took a nose-dive into depression.

What neither Kevin nor his parents yet realised was how the ambulance had reached Kevin so quickly that night. It was not a friendly passer-by, as Mr. Chuck possibly thought, but the last person on earth Kevin thought would help him – Tony Fowler.

As the gang ran off down the road after Kevin's fall, it was Tone who hung back at the corner, waiting to see Kevin get up. It was Tone who felt the nagging fear at the back of his mind. What if Kevin wasn't all right? What if he was badly hurt? – or even dead? The fun of the evening had evaporated for Tone and he no longer wanted to catch up with the gang on their laughing way up the street. But what could he do? Go back and help Kevin? Not likely! The creep had more or less deserved it, hadn't he? But he couldn't just leave him there, could he?

18

Suddenly, across the street, his eyes met the answer – a public call-box. Yes! That was the way out of his dilemma. Phone for an ambulance but don't give his name – that way he could make sure Kevin was looked after if he was hurt without him having to do the Good Samaritan bit. He checked that the gang weren't looking for him, then quickly crossed the street and entered the phone box.

Looking back afterwards, Tone couldn't be sure whether his feverish haste was fear of the gang discovering what he was doing or guilt over the way Kevin had been treated. But his fingers fumbled clumsily with the old-fashioned dial.

'Emergency. Which service do you require?' came the operator's coolly efficient voice.

'Eh? Oh, I want an ambulance, quick!' said Tone, flustering.

'Hold on, caller, I'm putting you through.'

'Ambulance service. Can I help you?' came another voice.

'Yeh! I want an ambulance, quick. There's a bloke lying on the pavement in Germaine Street – 'e looks bad,' explained Tone, who by now had recovered his composure.

'Can I have your name please?' said the voice.

'What? No, I'm not doing that. Just come quick!' Tone shouted before he rang off. He quickly looked round. No-one around still – good! He left the phone box hurriedly and ran to rejoin the gang before they wondered where he'd gone. He'd done his bit for Chuck now, more than the weed deserved, but Tone's conscience was eased by knowing that Kevin wouldn't be left there all night. The ambulance should be half-way there by now.

Nevertheless, Tone was in a thoughtful mood the rest of the evening and didn't share the gang's high spirits. He couldn't get Chuck out of his mind. He had hated him from the first day Kevin arrived at Wood End, when the new boy had grassed on him in Reynold's Science lesson and got him a detention. Then his resentment grew when Kevin wheedled his way into the gang and even outdid them all that day they went shoplifting. But then there was that other day – here Tone inwardly shuddered at the memory – when he let go of Kevin's dog and it dashed to its death under a car. He didn't mean it to happen – the stupid dog had suddenly jerked away from his hold – and of course he felt bad about it. And then he teased Kevin about it the next week – that was a rotten trick, he knew – and Tone even disliked himself for that.

He couldn't blame Kevin for hating him and the gang and breaking with them. He had never really fitted anyway. But Tone had noticed that soon afterwards Kevin had changed towards him. He never got friendly with Tone but once or twice Kevin had spoken civilly to him as if he no longer held a grudge against Tone. Maybe it's just because he's a weed – I'd never forgive anyone who did that to me, he thought. It was about the time Chuck got all religious and started hanging about with that Christian Union lot. Still I don't see what that has to do with it.

These and other similar thoughts spoiled the rest of Tone's Saturday night and he went to bed grumpy and fed up. Why should thinking about Kevin Chuck spoil his fun? He had a right to enjoy himself, didn't he? And if a weed like Chuck got hurt in the process, well that was hard luck. It wasn't Tone's fault. That was the firm resolution Tone stuck to throughout his fitful sleeping hours.

# 3

# Relapse

The next week at Wood End started like any other, but it wasn't long before rumours started about the accident to Kevin. Stories varied from Kevin falling off his bike and bumping his head to him having been beaten near to death and needing a long operation in hospital. Different people knew different versions of the story, of course. Gav and his mates were very ready to recount their Saturday night exploits against Kevin, adding their own gory embellishments for effect. Ginger was able to redress the balance, somewhat, by telling what he and his mum knew from the Chucks. Kevin was still at home recovering, so couldn't give the first-hand version of all that had happened to him. But even he didn't know about one piece of the jigsaw, how the ambulance had arrived. That only Tony could tell, and he was keeping very quiet about it.

Everyone was asking everyone else what happened that Monday morning and Tone was inevitably caught up in it all, being part of the gang. His interest was rather different from most people's, for, to his credit, he wanted to know how Kevin was recovering. He wouldn't admit it to himself, but his restless nights had given him a conscience, something he didn't live easily with. So he approached the boy who, he felt sure, would know something about Kevin's condition.

'Oi! Page! Over 'ere!' he called out to Darren when he spotted him at break time. 'What's this I heard about Chuck?' Tone tried to sound casual.

'As if you didn't know,' replied Darren scornfully. 'You were there, weren't you?'

'Yeh, I know that, but what happened to him after?'

'Huh! Fat lot you care! But if you must know, Ginger told me he came home from hospital yesterday and he's got to rest for a couple of days. They don't think it's concussion, so he'll be all right, no thanks to you!'

'Listen, Page. I'm not saying Chuck didn't deserve what he got but I wanna set the record straight. It was an accident, him getting knocked out – he tripped, didn't 'e, and banged 'is head. You can tell 'im from me, we didn't want it to end up like it did.'

'I find that hard to believe, Fowler. You and your gang are just a load of bullies. I wouldn't be surprised if you planned the whole thing, just to get revenge on Kevin because he's not one of your gang any more.'

'Look here, Page. You watch what you're saying.' Tone's temper was rising so that he blurted out, 'How do you think the ambulance got there, by magic?'

Immediately Tone realised he had said too much, as the look of wonder and realisation spread over Darren's face. He turned on his heel and strode off before Darren could question him further.

That comment sparked off a small explosion in Darren's mind, however, as he pondered on the mind-boggling implications of Tone's admission.

'Because that must mean that he was the one who called the ambulance, mustn't it?' he explained to Ginger, as they walked home from school that afternoon.

'I suppose so,' said Ginger, 'but why would he want to do that?'

'I dunno. Pang of conscience maybe, though I can hardly believe it of someone like Fowler.'

'Maybe you're right. My mum says there's some good in everyone, but I'm not so sure. Daley and his gang make my blood boil, especially after what they did to Kevin. But maybe you're right. Why else would Fowler call an ambulance?'

The question was still unresolved in their minds when

they turned the corner of Link Lane and looked for No. 28, home of the Chuck family. They had agreed beforehand to call round on Kevin to see how he was and cheer him up a bit. Mrs. Chuck was not long in answering their ring at the green-painted council house door and her face broke into a welcoming smile as she recognised Ginger.

'Can we see Kevin, please, Mrs. Chuck?' said Ginger.

'Yes, of course, Andy,' said Mrs. Chuck. 'Come in, and your friend.'

'Oh, this is Darren.' Ginger introduced him as they moved into the hallway.

'Well, Kevin's up in his room. He'll be so pleased to see you. He's starting to get bored already – even wants to go back to school tomorrow.'

'He's better then, is he?' asked Darren.

'Oh, much! The doctor came this morning and said he can get up and do what he wants, more or less. Go up and see him; you know his room, don't you Andy? I'll bring up some tea later.'

They trooped upstairs to find Kevin engrossed in one of his fishing magazines.

'Hiya, Kev! How ya doing? Thought you'd be like an Eygptian mummy – all bandages,' joked Ginger.

'Sorry to disappoint you,' laughed Kevin and his spirits lifted at the sight of the two friendly faces. The next half hour flew past as they chatted and joked and Kevin forgot the nightmare of Saturday night. They shared the events of the school day and even laughed over some of the rumours flying around about Kevin.

'Even Fowler was asking after you, Kev,' said Darren. 'Wanted to know how you were.'

Kevin's brow darkened. 'I never want to speak to him again,' he said in a mood of thunder. 'I'm surprised that you did.'

'Yes, I know how you feel, Kev,' said Darren, 'and I'd feel the same in your shoes. But he did say that he wanted you to know it was an accident, you being knocked out.'

'So what?' retorted Kevin. 'That's no excuse. It would never have happened if they hadn't started beating me up.'

'Yes, but there's something you don't know,' chipped in Ginger. 'He more or less admitted to Darren that it was he who called the ambulance.'

'What? I don't believe it,' was Kevin's reply.

'It's true, Kevin. He seemed to be sorry for what had happened,' added Darren.

'Frightened, more like, of what would happen to him if the police found out. I hate him and I'll never forgive him for what he did to me.'

'Kevin!' said Ginger, shocked. 'That's not like you. You don't really mean that, do you? Remember what Mr. Jenkins said at CU about the prodigal son?'

'Oh, shut up, Ginger!' said Kevin, as Ginger's remark touched a raw nerve. It was fortunate that Mrs. Chuck entered at that moment with the promised cups of tea, and the conversation was dropped for the rest of the visit. Soon Kevin's visitors left, with the assurance from Mrs. Chuck that he'd soon be rejoining them at school.

Kevin returned to Wood End on Wednesday, but it was a different Kevin Chuck from the one who had left it the previous Friday. Last week he had been happy, looking forward to the weekend, and confident about life in general. Now an empty blackness had overtaken his spirit and his mind was plagued with tormenting doubts and questions.

But to begin with, his return was a triumphal one, everyone wanting to know what had happened and which of the rumours was closest to the truth. Kevin enjoyed being the focus of attention and basked in the mixture of sympathy and admiration he was evoking. He once glimpsed Tone out of the corner of his eye and studiously ignored him.

'I'll bet he hates me because everyone's friends with me at the moment,' he thought to himself. 'Good! That'll even things up a bit and the feeling's mutual.'

Kevin and Tone avoided each other for the rest of that week, but far from dissipating Kevin's feelings, his anger grew as he nursed his bitterness and resentment. Why should he have to suffer at the hands of scum like Fowler? If the chance came he'd make him pay for it, someday. And as for Ginger and his talk of forgiveness, that was only for good Christians like him. Kevin wasn't at all sure that he fitted into that category any more, and anyway, God had let him down, hadn't he? There was no more point in praying to a God who didn't care, was there? Besides, he remembered enough from Mr. Jenkins' talk to know that if he couldn't forgive Tony Fowler, then God wouldn't forgive him. He'd failed as a Christian so there wasn't much point in trying to be one any more, was there?

The weekend did nothing to lessen Kevin's black mood. Somehow he didn't feel like going to his church's youth fellowship meeting and the fact that Ginger had to go out with his mother only deepened Kevin's self-imposed loneliness. Monday morning actually brought some relief from the tedium as the familiar school routine restarted. His grumpy moroseness was still evident on his face and he was quite glad that most of his class ignored him at registration. So he was rather taken aback when Tone approached him quietly and somewhat sheepishly.

'Sorry about your accident, Chuck. Glad you're all right now,' he said to Kevin in a subdued voice, hoping that none of the class would notice his conciliatory gesture. If this got out, his macho image would be severely dented.

Kevin recovered from his surprise. 'What do you mean – accident? It was your fault, Fowler – you're a swine

25

and a bully. I hope someone does it to you one day!'

Kevin's retort, on a rising tide of indignation, stung Tone to an equally vindictive reply. 'You're lucky you didn't get worse from us, Chuck. If you hadn't chickened out and taken a dive we'd have left you for dead!'

By this time the two boys were shouting and glaring at each other and the rest of the room had suddenly hushed to listen, just in time to hear Kevin's venomous outburst.

'I hate you, Fowler, and I'll get even with you one day. Get out of my sight and crawl back into the woodwork!'

There was a stunned silence at the viciousness of Kevin's last words, but as Tone prepared to launch a verbal and physical attack, the entrance of Mr. Green, their form tutor, prevented it.

Nevertheless, there was much scandalised whispering amongst the class and news of the confrontation soon spread amongst the fourth years, with raised eyebrows in some quarters at Kevin's out-of-character behaviour.

So the enmity between Kevin and Tone which had been simmering beneath the surface for several months, was now an open feud. Strangely, it was Kevin who was glad about it and was almost wishing Tone would give him an excuse for a fight in the playground. Tone gave him no such excuse though, contenting himself only with angry and hateful stares which Kevin returned with interest. It was like the calm before the storm which almost the whole fourth year were expecting to break any moment. It did break, but in a way which no-one had anticipated.

Kevin's moodiness affected everything and everyone around him that week. His parents noticed it at home but could get nothing out of him except the occasional grunt to break the loud silences. His friends noticed it but couldn't cheer him up, no matter how they tried. Even his teachers began to notice his apathy in lessons and could instil no enthusiasm into him. His homework suffered too and on Thursday Kevin realised that his history essay was due in. He resorted to his old dodge from the third year, copying someone else's, and who better to choose than good old Steve Dodds? Kevin approached him at breaktime.

'Steve, can I borrow your history essay for old Austin? She'll kill me if I don't hand it in today.'

'Have my ears deceived me?' replied Steve in mock disbelief. 'The great Kevin Chuck wanting to copy my homework? You haven't done that since the third year. I thought you were too high and mighty for the likes of me.'

'I don't know what gave you that idea,' said Kevin, blushing. 'I only asked as a favour. If you don't want to lend me yours. . . .'

'Oh no! Here you are, help yourself,' said Steve, diving into his bag to fish out his essay. 'I don't mind helping you out, but I thought you'd turned all religious now.'

'What difference does that make?' said Kevin, immediately on the defensive.

'Well, I thought you Christians were supposed to be honest and didn't believe in things like cheating and copying your homework. You stopped doing it when you joined the Christian Union last year and you told me then that you were always going to do your own work from then on. A fine Christian you've turned out to be!'

The force of Steve's words hit Kevin like a slap on the cheek. Words to justify himself flew to his mind – bitter, sarcastic, angry words. But somewhere deep inside he recognised the truth of Steve's taunt, and his words as mere excuses. He stared at Steve, open-mouthed, like a fish out of water, searching for something appropriate to say. Unfortunately for Kevin, Lyn had overheard the conversation and took advantage of the pause to join in.

'I think all religious people are hypocrites. Our vicar's always drinking and smoking. And what about you, Kevin? A right mouthful you gave our Tone the other day – very strong! Doesn't the Bible say something about turning the other cheek and loving your enemies?'

Kevin tried to outstare the brazen look of Lyn's brown eyes, but he couldn't deny the accuracy of her Bible knowledge.

'I didn't know Tone was using girls to stick up for him now,' said Kevin, as the only retort he could think of.

'Tone doesn't need me to stick up for him, but I think he's right,' glared Lyn. 'You're an upstart, Kevin, and you don't fit in. Your family come here from wherever it was, take up a job and council house that someone else could have had, and then start behaving like you expect us all to bow down to you. You're so superior!'

'Is that what you all think?' gasped Kevin.

'Well it's true, isn't it, Mr. Clever? You even tried to convert me and Sarah the other day, didn't you, you stuck-up prig?'

'Oh shut up, Lyn, you do go on,' broke in Steve. 'You've got a chip on your shoulder about religion, so cut it out. But you must admit, Kevin, that Tone's got a right to feel sore. I know your dog got killed, but you've never let him forget it, and it's no wonder he says things like you should go back to yokels' land. Your dad's got a good job, and his dad's been out of work for over a year.'

Kevin was overwhelmed by the force of this attack from his classmates and from the onslaught of such new ideas. He wanted only to escape, and with a parting shot to Steve of, 'Well keep your rotten essay, then!' he skulked out of the room, taking his embarrassment and misery with him.

That evening at 28 Link Lane, Mr. and Mrs. Chuck talked feelingly about their son.

'He's been like a bear with a sore head the past ten days,' moaned Mr. Chuck. 'I'm beginning to think that accident knocked him out in more ways than one.'

'Yes, and he'd been so cheerful too, before. He'd really been looking forward to the fourth year and he was working so hard. Now all he does is mope in front of the telly all evening,' fretted Mrs. Chuck. 'I can't get a word out of him about what's wrong.'

'I must admit that I haven't been paying much attention to him recently,' added Mr. Chuck. 'I thought he'd settled down at school after that terrible start last year, and with the dog getting run over.'

'I don't think he ever really got over her death,' sighed Mrs. Chuck.

'Oh, I think you're exaggerating, dear. But you've made me think,' mused Mr. Chuck. 'I wonder if there's something we could do, after all.'

While this conversation was taking place, upstairs in his bedroom Kevin was staring forlornly at the blank wall. It seemed as if he hadn't a friend left in the world; he'd lost them all by his surly and obstinate behaviour. Tone hated him, Steve despised him, and he'd shocked Ginger and Darren by his angry outbursts. But greater than all these, Kevin knew he'd let God down. He'd done all the things a Christian shouldn't, and done it in front of everyone. What would they think of him now? More important, what would they think of his religion, and God? Would God ever be able to forgive Kevin?

'Lord, help me,' he suddenly blurted out, and then the bottled-up thoughts came rushing out. 'God, I've really blown it. I've been useless and messed it up completely. I've said some terrible things and been full of hate and feeling sorry for myself. I hate myself and I know you must too. And I shouldn't really be a Christian any more, Lord, and I'll understand if that's what you want.' He paused. Did he really mean these next few words? 'But Lord, I am sorry. Can you forgive me? I don't really think you can, Lord, but if you do, then please send a sign or something, so that I'll know I can believe in you again. I want to believe that you care, Lord. Do you really?'

# 4

## Rusty

Kevin woke the next morning strangely subdued. He hadn't been aware of even falling asleep last night. He felt now drained of emotion but with a sense of peace he had not known yesterday. It was as he was washing that he remembered his prayer and the desperate words he had spoken. He didn't know if God would answer and he certainly couldn't see how, but he was quietly aware that he didn't have to worry about that side of things.

His day at school was, thankfully, a quiet one. He kept well out of Tone's way and minded his own business. Others seemed content to let him alone and although he would perhaps have welcomed a friendly word from Ginger or Darren, even they seemed to avoid him, perhaps fearing another angry scene. Kevin couldn't blame them.

One thought did cross his mind that day, however, and it was a chance remark Steve had made during that argument the previous day. Something about Tone's dad being out of work – for over a year, hadn't Steve said? That rang a bell in Kevin's mind. Hadn't Tone told him the same thing on his first day? So it must be true. But why should that be important? What had it got to do with Kevin? He didn't owe Tony Fowler any thought or consideration, did he? And even if he did there was nothing he could do about it, was there?

Friday afternoon dragged as usual and everyone was glad when the final bell whirred its piercing scream down the corridors. Everyone raced for the doors, running downstairs and along passageways, ignoring teachers' calls to walk, racing across the playground in a haphazard criss-cross pattern to merge into a jostling mass at the school gates. The lower years were first, outstripping the senior school who preferred to maintain an appearance of dignity as they too hurried towards the start of the weekend's freedom.

Kevin walked through his own back door to find his mother waiting with a cup of tea for him. That and the odd smile she gave him told Kevin that something was up.

'Drink your tea up, Kevin, love,' she said, almost as soon as he'd sat down.

'Why? What's the hurry?' inquired Kevin, intrigued.

'We're going out again. Dad wants us to meet him at a quarter past four.'

'What on earth for? And besides, he doesn't finish work until five,' said Kevin, even more mystified.

'He's leaving work early today, and you'll find out why later on,' said Mrs. Chuck, a conspiratorial grin on her face.

She would divulge no more information to him so it was a baffled and somewhat annoyed Kevin who accompanied his mother to the High Street to wait for his father's car. Just when he'd been looking forward to a relaxing hour in front of the telly, this had to happen. But he couldn't help feeling curious.

'Hello, love. Sorry I'm late,' called Mr. Chuck as they climbed into the battered Ford Cortina. 'The traffic's murder, even at four o'clock.'

'That's all right, dear. We've only been waiting ten minutes,' said Mrs. Chuck.

'What's this all about, Dad?' said Kevin. 'Mum won't tell me a thing.'

'I'll explain on the way, Kevin. Just let's get out of this traffic first,' said his father.

So they travelled in silence at first, weaving their way in and out of the ever-increasing traffic flow. Eventually they cleared the worst of it and accelerated towards an area of town Kevin knew little about.

'We're going to see a mate of mine at work, Kevin,' explained his father. 'He lives a fair way out, so I thought I'd leave work early so we can get back in time for tea.'

'But why do I have to come? You can see your friends without me, can't you?' complained Kevin.

'Ah! But you see, he's got something you might be interested in,' smiled Mr. Chuck, with the same secretive grin his mother had used earlier. Kevin could get nothing more out of him until they arrived.

'Hello, Alan! You found us then. Come in!' said a big burly man who answered the door when they knocked.

'Hello, Geoff. Yes, your instructions were very good. This is my wife, Doreen, and this is Kevin.'

'Pleased to meet you,' said Geoff. 'Well, I expect you'd like to meet her straight away, and the young 'uns.'

'Yes please,' said Mr. Chuck, and they followed Geoff through the hall into the kitchen.

'Funny way to talk about your wife and children,' thought Kevin.

It all sounded very strange and he still hadn't guessed the purpose of their visit when Geoff announced. 'Here we are. Kevin, meet Sophie.'

Kevin had the shock of his life. There, staring up at him with big brown eyes and floppy red ears was a beautiful Red Setter. The likeness between her and Judy brought a sharp prick of emotion behind his eyes even after all these months.

'And these are her litter,' went on Geoff, 'three dogs and a bitch.' And in an adjoining basket, frolicking and tumbling over each other, were four adorable young puppies. So this was what it was all about. Kevin was speechless.

'Which one would you like, Kevin?' said Mr. Chuck.

'They're two months old, so you can take one away with you now,' explained Geoff.

Kevin was in a daze and bent down to the playful puppies. One of them immediately came to him and licked his hand, making his decision easy.

'Looks like that one's chosen you, son,' smiled Geoff, and Kevin smiled his agreement. He picked up the puppy.

'Thanks, Dad.' He wanted to say more, but words failed him. Mr. and Mrs. Chuck didn't mind. The look on Kevin's face said it all. Kevin floated on air back to the car and it was a more united family that returned home that evening.

'We've still got Judy's basket and leads up in the loft, so you can use those,' said Mrs. Chuck. 'We'll get him a new blanket though.'

'You'll have to train him properly,' warned Mr. Chuck. 'What are you going to call him?'

'I don't know yet, Dad. I'll think of something,' said Kevin, dreamily oblivious of everything except his new possession climbing all over him in the back seat.

His delight continued all through a happy tea-time and he had lost all track of time when there was an unexpected ring at the front door.

'I'll go, Mum,' said Kevin, and found the familiar smiling face of Ginger on the doorstep.

'Hello, Kev. Wondered if you were coming to YPF tonight.'

'Is it time already?' gasped Kevin. 'I never realised. Hang on a minute.' All his suspicions of Ginger avoiding him at school melted away at the sight of the cheery freckled face grinning at him.

'Mum! Dad! It's Ginger. You don't mind if I go out, do you? Will you be able to look after the puppy?'

'I expect we might manage that,' said a beaming Mr. Chuck. 'We've had enough practice in the past.'

'Look out! He's got out!' shouted Mrs. Chuck and they tore after him into the hall where they found him busy licking Ginger's face. There was laughter and a sheepish Ginger picked up the puppy and handed him back to Kevin.

'You didn't tell me you were getting another dog, Kevin,' smiled Ginger.

'I didn't know myself till this evening,' explained Kevin, 'And I've just thought of a great name for him. "Ginger", as he seems to like you so much.'

'Bit confusing, isn't it? I don't want to be mistaken for a dog,' laughed Ginger.

'What about "Rusty"?' offered Mrs. Chuck.

'That's it!' beamed Kevin. 'Well done, Mum!' and he even gave her a kiss.

As Kevin set off with Ginger for the weekly YPF meeting, Mr. Chuck turned to Doreen, 'That's the brightest I've seen him for a long time.'

'Yes, it certainly worked, your idea of the puppy. Well done, dear,' said Mrs. Chuck as hand in hand they turned back into the house to tackle the washing up together.

Kevin chatted happily to Ginger all about his new pet as they walked down to the church hall and Ginger couldn't help commenting on it.

'You seem much brighter this evening, Kevin.'

'Yes, I've been pretty sore at everything, I know,' said Kevin ruefully. 'Until last night I didn't really care, but then I realised how rotten I'd been and also how much I'd let God down.'

'So what happened last night?'

'I guess I finally swallowed my pride and said sorry,' said Kevin, 'I didn't know whether God would forgive me, though.'

'Of course he will,' said Ginger. 'Remember the prodigal son?'

'Yes,' smiled Kevin, 'but I also asked him for a sign. . . .'

He broke off, realisation dawning on him as he thought of the past two happy hours.

35

'What sign?' asked Ginger.

'Of course! I asked God for a sign that he still cares about me and the next day I get a new puppy. That must be an answer to prayer.'

'Wow! That's great, Kev. But you look surprised. Of course God answers prayer. Have you only just found that out?' he teased. Kevin cuffed him in reply and they ran and laughed the rest of the way.

Table tennis was in full swing when they entered and Kevin looked forward to his turn to play. He had only started playing a few months ago at YPF but already he had discovered a talent for the game which others were beginning to recognise too. Darren approached Kevin as the game drew to a close.

'Fancy a game, Kevin? It's my turn next. I'll play you if you like.'

'But I'd never beat you,' said Kevin. Darren was the undisputed unofficial champion of YPF.

'That doesn't matter, does it? You never know, I might let you get a few points off me,' Darren joked.

'OK, then,' agreed Kevin, and they took up opposite ends of the table as the game finished. After a knock-up, Darren quickly built up a lead with his fast serve. Kevin took some time getting used to his opponent's smashes and quick hitting but gradually pulled himself back into the game with solid defensive play and accurate placing. The rallies became longer and errors began to creep into Darren's normally assured performance. As the game reached its climax, Kevin's score edged closer to Darren's. The comeback couldn't last, though, and Darren finally won 21–18 after Kevin just failed to find the table.

'Well played, Kevin. You're much better than I thought you would be,' said Darren generously.

'Thanks. It was pretty difficult trying to get your serve back,' admitted Kevin.

'We'll have to play again. At this rate you'll soon be

beating me.'

They bought two Cokes from the tuck shop and sat watching the next game. Suddenly Kevin's eyes shot to the doorway as through it walked the daunting figure of Terry Boxall, the biggest, and possibly the meanest member of Gav's gang.

Kevin nudged Darren in the ribs. 'That's Boxall, from school,' he gasped. 'What's he doing here?'

'Oh, he came last week when you weren't here,' said Darren. 'He used to come some time ago too, before he teamed up with Gavin Daley.'

'Oh, yes! I remember now,' said Kevin. He remembered, too, the time when Terry had got caught shoplifting and Derek, the YPF leader, had gone round and chatted to his parents and generally helped sort the problems out. Kevin now had mixed feelings about seeing him there. A day earlier he'd have either ignored him or made some insulting comment but now it was all different. Kevin knew now that God had forgiven him and that this was his chance to make amends. He got up and wandered over to arrive at the tuckshop simultaneously with Terry.

'Hello, Terry, nice to see you,' he began.

Terry turned and stared as if he'd seen a ghost. Then he relaxed and put on his usual brazen manner. 'Watcha, Chuck. I didn't expect to see you here, but then I forgot – you're one of the Jesus creeps, aren't you?'

'Yes, if you like,' laughed Kevin, determined not to let Terry needle him. 'Can I buy you a Coke?' he offered magnanimously.

'You must be joking!' was Terry's retort. 'I don't want any favours from you, Chuck, especially not after the way you spoke to Tone this week. I don't want anything to do with you religious lot. I just come here for the games. I'll stick to my friends and you stick to yours.'

Kevin had nothing to say in reply and returned crestfallen to his seat. He'd tried to make amends for his angry words at school but had just been snubbed for it. All his new found elation suddenly vanished like the air from a popped balloon. Fortunately Derek, the leader, saw what happened, and sat down beside Kevin.

'What's the matter, Kevin?'

'It's Terry Boxall, he told me to mind my own business when I was only trying to be friendly,' explained Kevin. Bit by bit Derek coaxed the whole story from Kevin, the beating-up, the hate and bitterness, the angry words spoken to Tone, and Kevin's prayer for forgiveness.

'Listen, Kevin,' Derek finally said. 'God longs to forgive us, but that doesn't mean that other people do. Terry and Tone still feel angry towards you, and you can't expect them to change overnight. They don't know God's forgiveness like you do. You must show tonight that you have no hard feelings towards Terry, that you are big enough to forgive him. And with Tone you need to take the first step.'

'You mean, say sorry to him?' asked Kevin.

'Yes, that, and something more, if you can. Something definite to show him that it's not just words – you really do want to heal the terrible hurts in your relationship. But I haven't a clue what that could be – you'll have to work that out.' And with that, Derek was dragged away to sort out a dispute over the rules of snooker.

'OK. I'll try it, Derek,' he said softly to himself. It wasn't easy, but Kevin refused the rest of the evening to be riled by Terry and continued to be as friendly as he could be. On the way home, though, he pondered over Derek's other advice. Do something for Tone. But what? Suddenly it clicked. What had been nagging away at the back of his mind all day – Tone's dad without a job. Maybe that was the answer, if only he could see what to do. But just as Kevin now knew for sure that God had forgiven him, he knew too that God had put the thought in his mind and was gently showing him the next step.

'And thanks a million, Lord, for that sign,' prayed Kevin, as he hurried home to Rusty.

# 5

## Ask for a miracle

'Where's Dad?' yawned Kevin, as he sleepily emerged for breakfast the next morning.

'In the garden, working,' said Mrs. Chuck. 'We can't all stay in bed all morning, you know. There's the puppy to be looked after as well.'

'All right, Mum, don't nag. I'm going to buy some dog food and things this morning. His name's Rusty by the way – had you forgotten?'

'No, of course I hadn't. He's been running round my heels and tripping me up all through breakfast.' Inwardly, though, she was pleased at the way the puppy had brought joy and laughter back to their house.

Kevin found his father sweeping up the leaves.

'Morning, son. Trained that new dog of yours yet?'

'Not yet. Dad, can I ask you a favour?'

'What? After I've just bought you that puppy!' joked Mr. Chuck.

'No, seriously, Dad. It's about a boy at school. His dad's been out of work for over a year and I wondered if you knew of any jobs going where you work.'

'Oh I see,' Mr. Chuck looked thoughtful. 'Well, jobs are like gold dust round here, son. But I'll see what I can do and put in a good word for this bloke if his son's a friend of yours. What's his name and what's his trade?'

'His name's Mr. Fowler, and he used to be a brickie, so I guess he could do anything to do with building or labouring,' offered Kevin. 'I wrote his address and telephone number down here,' and Kevin offered the piece of paper. Little did Mr. Chuck know that Kevin had only found it out by looking in the phone book and that neither Tone nor his dad knew anything about Kevin's gesture, and would hardly be grateful if they did. What would Kevin's dad say if he knew that Tone was one of the gang who beat him up?

'All right, son. Leave it on the dressing table. I'll see what I can do next week, but no promises, mind!' he warned.

'Thanks, Dad. I knew you would,' and Kevin rushed off, leaving Mr. Chuck as pleased as his wife at the upturn in Kevin's spirits.

Kevin's weekend was a happy and lively one; Rusty proved to be quite a handful and needed constant attention and guidance. Kevin found himself mopping up puddles on the kitchen floor as well as making sure Rusty stayed indoors. There were vet's visits to be arranged, and things to buy, as well as the fun of having a very playful, mischievous puppy around. In no time at all it was Monday morning and back to school. How different this Monday was to the last! Kevin actually looked forward to getting back to work, to seeing his friends again, and to trying to make up for his behaviour of last week. He knew too that that meant apologising to Tone for what he said, a prospect Kevin did not enjoy and he was relieved that no opportunity presented itself that first morning. One thing that puzzled him was the absence of Ginger. He was perfectly all right at church on Sunday and it was unlike him to miss school for no reason.

He was not left wondering for long. He arrived home from school to find Ginger and Mrs. Webb sitting round the kitchen table with his mother, all drinking tea. Mrs. Webb looked rather off-colour and there was a tense and anxious atmosphere hovering over them all.

'Hi, Ginger! Hello, Mrs. Webb!' Kevin wanted to say more but the looks they all gave him stopped him in his tracks. Mrs. Chuck explained.

'Kevin, love, Mrs. Webb came over to ask us a favour. Her mother's been taken poorly – she's had a stroke –

and Mrs. Webb, Pauline, is going up to Nottingham to look after her. So she came to ask us if we'd mind putting up Andy for a week while she's away. I said of course we would and I didn't think you'd mind.'

'Mind?' exclaimed Kevin. 'That'd be great, Ginger!'

Ginger's face lit up and Mrs. Webb forced a weak smile. 'It's very good of you all. I've been running round all day trying to sort things out and getting Andy some clean clothes. He's been very helpful.'

Ginger blushed. Mrs. Chuck broke in, 'Now, don't you worry about a thing, Pauline. Andy will be quite all right with us. You get along now or you'll miss your train.'

So within ten minutes of Kevin arriving home, Mrs. Webb had left, amid many reassurances and good wishes, and Kevin had his best friend staying with him for a week.

'Right now, you two,' said Mrs. Chuck in a business-like manner, 'when you've finished your tea you can both bring Andy's things upstairs. You'll have to sleep on a camp bed, Andy, but I hope you won't mind that, and I thought you'd like to sleep in the same room as Kevin.'

'Yes, that'll be fine, thanks, Mrs. Chuck, but do call me Ginger. Everyone else does – well, everyone except Mum that is.'

'Well, as I'm not your mother, Ginger it is,' laughed Mrs. Chuck and with all nervousness gone they good-humouredly proceeded to settle Ginger in.

Little homework was done that evening as Kevin and Ginger chatted, watched TV together and found constant amusement in Rusty's antics. Mr. Chuck suffered their noisy chatter with patient tolerance but insisted that bedtime was still at a reasonable hour. Sleep is hard to find, though, especially when you can chat and swap jokes. So it was a bleary-eyed pair that Mrs. Chuck woke at eight the next morning.

'Come on, you two. You'll be late for school if you don't get a move on. You're usually up half an hour ago, Kevin. Breakfast is on the table and I expect you down in fifteen minutes.'

Her words stirred them both into getting up and Kevin staggered to the bathroom. He washed and dressed more quickly now as he realised he was going to have less time for reading his Bible and praying. He sat on his bed and read the allotted passage for the day but it was difficult to concentrate on it with Ginger still moving around getting dressed. In the end, they just made it together to breakfast on time and from then on the busy process of getting to school dominated everything else.

Kevin was somewhat puzzled and frustrated when exactly the same thing happened the next morning. He had always looked up to Ginger as a better Christian than himself and had assumed that Ginger would spend twice as long each day reading his Bible and praying. It was a shock to discover the truth and at first Kevin didn't like to ask Ginger about it.

Tuesday lunchtime had been the Christian Union meeting when they had discussed the meaning of friendships and the need to forgive someone 'seventy times seven', as Jesus once said. Kevin was reminded that he still needed to apologise to Tone and wished he could have done it then and there, but Tone was away that day. Rumour had it that he'd taken the rest of the week off to go motor bike racing with his older brother.

It was Ginger who reminded Kevin of the meeting that night as they lay in bed.

'Hey, Kevin. You know what Mr. Jenkins said at CU today about forgiving our friends and praying for them?'

'Yes,' said Kevin, half asleep.

'Well, why don't we pray for them now? I'd like to pray for Justin in my class. He's always making fun of me because I go to the CU. And I ought to pray for Mum too, and for Gran, that she'll get better.'

'OK,' agreed Kevin. 'I'd like to pray for Darren as he's got a cold, and I suppose I ought to pray for Tone too, that I'll be able to forgive him.'

So together they prayed for friends and people they knew. Ginger took the lead and Kevin was impressed by the way Ginger seemed able to talk to God just like he was Ginger's dad or even like a best friend. A quarter of an hour passed as quickly as thinking before they had finished.

'That was great,' said Kevin, when they finally opened their eyes.

'You sound surprised,' said Ginger. 'Don't you like praying?'

'Well yes, I suppose so,' said Kevin, unsure. 'I mean, I try to pray every day. I've been wanting to ask you – you didn't read your Bible today or yesterday. I thought we were supposed to as Christians.'

'Yes, you're right,' admitted Ginger. 'I do try to have a time for talking to God every day but I'm not very good at it. You seem much better than me at keeping it up.'

'I don't know about that,' blushed Kevin, 'but when you do pray you seem to be able to keep at it for much longer than I do.'

'Well, I don't know about that,' laughed Ginger, 'but when I know how much God loves me and longs to be my best friend and the father that I never had, it seems easy just to sit and chat to him.'

'If you say so,' said Kevin, unconvinced. It had never occurred to him to regard God in that way – it seemed irreverent. But Ginger certainly knew how to pray in a way that he didn't.

'Anyway, we'd better get some sleep. It's gone eleven,' said Kevin, glancing at the clock.

'Yeah. Goodnight, Kevin.'

'Goodnight, Ginger. And thanks. I enjoyed the praying.'

'So did I,' agreed Ginger as he yawned himself off to sleep.

The week flew past for Kevin and Ginger, both of them learning more about the other each day. Ginger became more regular in Bible reading and Kevin understood a little more about praying. They learned other things too. Ginger was rather fussy over his meals and annoyed Mrs. Chuck more than once by the food left on his plate. But he showed a surprising patience when it came to stopping Rusty chewing the furniture and mopping up his puddles everywhere. Patience was something Kevin lacked but he had a lot of practical skills that Ginger lacked and they spent an absorbing Friday evening servicing Ginger's bike which he fetched from home.

'Where shall we go tomorrow, then?' asked Ginger. It was already an unspoken agreement that a bike journey was planned.

'You know the area better than me,' said Kevin.

'All right. How about Banbury Reservoir? That's not too far and would get us back before dark.'

'Good idea. I'll ask Mum to make us a packed lunch.'

With the bikes ready checked and oiled, all that was needed was a fine sunny day. Nature was not so kind to them this time, however, and Saturday dawned dark and threatening. But the prospect of rain did not deter them and the freedom of the road was a strong call to two adventurous spirits. With only a delay to find their stored-away waterproofs they set off for the Woolwich ferry and the road north.

Soon after crossing the river, the threatened rain started to fall and they duly donned their riding capes. The skies opened soon afterwards and before long they were cycling in a steady downpour, rain attacking them mercilessly and finding all the leaks in their clothing. Conversation soon ceased; it was all they could do to stay upright and avoid the puddles and splashes of passing cars. Common sense might have told them to give up but by this time they were out of the shopping areas and onto the dual carriageway. There seemed nothing for it but to persevere and hope that the rain would lift by the time they reached their destination and stopped for lunch. Soon Kevin wished they hadn't.

It was as they rounded a bend that the accident happened. Ginger was leading when a car raced round from the opposite direction, hogging the middle of the road and giving scant consideration to the two cyclists. Ginger swerved to avoid the inevitable splash of water from the car's tyres, skidded on the wet surface, overbalanced and finally fell heavily on to his side.

Kevin's brakes screeched to a halt and he ran to Ginger.

'Ginger! Are you all right?'

'I think so. It's just my wrist,' said Ginger, grimacing.

'That stupid idiot in the car. He should look where he's going. Still it's not far now. Your bike seems all right. Can you carry on?'

'I don't think so, Kev. It's my wrist. It's darned painful.'

'Let's have a look, then.' Kevin took hold of Ginger's arm and gently moved the wrist but Ginger let out a yell of agony.

'Don't Kev. It's murder.'

Kevin stood nonplussed. He tried to think. They were a long way from home, too far to walk, but if Ginger couldn't cycle, what then? They weren't near any houses or shops and there was no-one around to help at all. Kevin gave up.

'Well, I don't know what we're going to do, Ginger. Looks like we're stuck,' said Kevin, as he felt the panic rising from the pit of his stomach.

'There's only one thing we can do, Kev. That's pray.'

'What? We haven't got time for things like that.' In truth, Kevin had never thought of it, though he didn't like to admit it.

'Come on, Kev. If we trust God, he'll look after us. All we've got to do is ask.'

'Well, OK, if you say so. You'd better do the praying though. I wouldn't know what to say,' admitted Kevin.

'Lord,' began Ginger, 'you know we're in a right mess. We're miles from anywhere and my wrist is agony. Please heal my wrist, Father, and take away the pain so that I can ride home with Kev.'

That's a daft prayer, thought Kevin. With his wrist in so much pain there's no way he can ride anywhere. But Ginger kept on praying, this time in a low voice so that Kevin couldn't hear. After a few minutes Ginger stopped and looked up.

'It's all right now, Kev. I think if we take it steady I'll be able to ride home with you.'

'But how? You were in agony, just now. You'll never make it!' exclaimed Kevin.

'Just let's try it, shall we? I asked God to take the pain away and he has. Come on! Get going and lead the way before I chicken out. And keep praying!'

Kevin was too bewildered to argue, so he got on his bike and started back home. Ginger rode delicately but steadily behind him, content to let Kevin set the pace and decide the route. Several times Kevin glanced back but Ginger was still there, white-faced but determined, and often Kevin would hear him praying in a quiet voice, though he couldn't make out the words.

'It must be a miracle,' thought Kevin two hours later when they finally turned into Link Lane. But that was the last time he had to think, for as soon as his parents saw them they hurried to change their wet clothes and rush Ginger down to the hospital.

Kevin and his parents waited restlessly in the outpatients department, crowded with victims of football and rugby injuries.

'The last time we were here,' recalled Mr. Chuck, 'we

were waiting to see you, Kevin. They'll soon be saving us a permanent place.'

Kevin smiled weakly at his father's joke. He just hoped that Ginger's arm was all right and that he hadn't done it any permanent damage by cycling all that way.

After what seemed like hours, Ginger emerged from the consulting room with a doctor in tow carrying a large envelope with 'X-Ray' clearly marked on it. Ginger gave Kevin the thumbs up sign before a nurse led him down the corridor to the plaster room. The doctor approached the trio.

'Good afternoon. I gather you are looking after Andrew Webb while his mother's away.'

'Yes, that's right, doctor,' replied Mr. Chuck.

'Well, I'm happy to tell you that he'll be fine. It was a clean break and once we've had it set he'll be on the mend in no time.'

'But how did he manage to cycle home with a broken wrist?' interrupted Kevin.

'That's impossible, young man. You must be mistaken,' said the doctor, his young brow furrowing at Kevin.

'But he did,' insisted Kevin. 'Two hours it took us.'

'All right, Kevin, that's enough,' warned his father. 'The doctor's got more important things to do than listen to your tales.'

Kevin would have protested but what was the use? He drifted out of the conversation. But how had Ginger managed to do it? He'd said he believed in the power of prayer, out there on the lonely road, when there was nothing else to help them, and it looked as if Ginger's faith had proved right. This time Kevin said it to himself with real meaning: 'It must have been a miracle!'

# 6

## Dancing and fighting

Mrs. Webb had quite a shock when she arrived home that Sunday night to find Ginger with his arm in plaster. Everyone soon reassured her, however, and Mrs. Chuck was on hand with a welcoming cup of coffee. She was obviously relieved to be home and pleased to see familiar faces. After a while Mrs. Chuck voiced the question they all wanted to ask.

'And how is your mother, Pauline?'

'She's much better, thanks. She's pulled through the stroke, and the hospital reckon she could live to a ripe old age. But it's been an exhausting week. They were quite prepared to let her come home and continue living on her own, even though I told them that I lived in London and that she had no neighbours she could rely on. I spent all week contacting Social Services and trying to get her into an old people's home, but all I managed to arrange was a daily visit from a home help, at least for the first few weeks.'

'Yes, I know, they can't get you out of hospital beds quick enough,' commiserated Mrs. Chuck. 'How is your mother taking it?'

'Oh, she's quite cheerful, and I was able to see her safely installed back home before I left. It's the least I could do for her after all she's done for me, but I wish I didn't live so far away. In fact I even wondered about arranging to go and live with Mum for a while.'

Ginger and Kevin looked at one another in horror. Ginger moving to Nottingham was the last thing either of them wanted.

'But I haven't made up my mind yet,' continued Mrs.

Webb, 'so we'll just wait and see. And now, young man, we'd better get you home so I can start nursing my other invalid relative.'

Monday morning saw Tone returning to school from his trial-biking interlude, with obvious reluctance written all over his face. Kevin hadn't forgotten his resolution to speak to him and thought this might be as good a time as any. His week with Ginger had taught him an important lesson for such crises, however, and he put it into practice straight away.

'Lord, please help me,' he muttered under his breath as he sauntered nonchalantly over to where Tone was sitting alone during their form period. As casually as he could he opened the conversation.

'Had a good time with the bikes, Tone?'

Tone looked up, a mixture of surprise and scorn on his face, 'Yeh,' he scowled, 'so what's it to you? I thought you never wanted to see me again.'

'Yes, I know. I wanted to speak to you about that.' Kevin took a deep breath. 'Look, I'm sorry I spoke to you the way I did. I was upset and I didn't mean it. I'd like you to forget it.' Kevin waited apprehensively for Tone's reaction. Surely it would be all right now.

'Look, Chuck, what you said before is fine with me. You don't wanna mix with me and I certainly don't want anything to do with your set. Let's leave it like that.'

Now it was Kevin's turn to feel hurt and he turned away in dismay. He'd done his best to make it up but Tone had turned his offer down flat. But at least Tone hadn't shouted at him so maybe there was hope yet. And if Kevin could find it in him to carry on praying for him, like Mr. Jenkins said. . . . Kevin turned away. There was no point in standing there when Tone obviously didn't want to talk. He walked back to his place, feeling rather deflated and at a loose end now. What was the time? Oh, still another ten minutes of boring form period

– but it was better than maths, at least. Maths! Maths meant maths homework, the problems he'd pored over at the weekend. He might as well get it out and check his answers again.

'Hey, Steve! You're in Harvey's maths set. What did you make of the homework?' he called out.

'Murder! It took me over half an hour,' replied Steve.

'You're lucky! It took me an hour. What did you make the answers then?' said Kevin.

'You're not trying to copy me again, are you?' joked Steve light-heartedly as he tossed over his exercise book.

'No, of course not. I just want to see if I've got the same as you.' Kevin was slow to appreciate the joke.

'It's all right. Don't get on your high horse!' said Steve, holding up his hands in mock horror. 'I was just wondering whether you're allowed to, or if your religious rules say "Thou shalt not look at someone else's homework",' he mocked.

Despite himself, Kevin was riled by Steve's taunt and immediately on the defensive. 'Don't be stupid!' he retorted. 'Just because I'm a Christian doesn't mean I'm any different from other people.'

'Doesn't it?' Steve pressed the matter. 'I thought there were all sorts of do's and don'ts, things you're not allowed to do and places you're not allowed to go.'

'That's rubbish!' said Kevin, unwisely. 'Like what?'

'Oh, I dunno,' said Steve vaguely, 'well, like smoking or drinking or going to discos, that sort of thing. You'd never be seen dead doing those.'

'Who says I wouldn't?' Kevin snapped. 'I've tried smoking and didn't like it – anyway, it's stupid burning money to ruin your health. And I drink sometimes at parties.'

'Bet you've never got drunk!'

'No, that's stupid too. You only puke up all over the place.'

'Everything's stupid to you, isn't it?' said Steve, exasperated. 'I suppose you think discos are stupid?'

'I never said that.'

'No, but I bet you've never been to one.'

'OK. So what?' said Kevin. He was still angry that Steve should regard him as an alien, a sort of religious ET.

'Well that proves my point. You don't go because your rules say "Thou shalt not". Either that or you're too scared,' Steve mocked.

'Who says I'm scared?' fumed Kevin. 'I'll go to any disco you like!'

Steve would have said more but at this point their form tutor looked up at the sound of Kevin's raised voice and tersely warned them to be quiet. Next minute the bell went and ended any opportunity to pursue the discussion.

Although Kevin's anger soon subsided, Steve had not forgotten Kevin's words and spent the rest of the day on a little scheme he was hatching.

On Wednesday he cornered Kevin. 'I've fixed it up then,' he said coolly.

'Fixed what up?' said Kevin, who had forgotten all about his bravado two days earlier.

'Our night at the disco. All set for Friday night down at the Youth Centre. They've got a visiting DJ coming.'

'I don't remember saying I was going anywhere,' said Kevin, puzzled.

'Yes, you did – on Monday. You said you'd come. You're not chickening out are you?' insinuated Steve.

'No, of course not,' said Kevin, rising to the bait of Steve's calculated jibe. 'It's just that I didn't realise you meant any particular disco.'

'Oh, yes. I've arranged it all. And I've fixed up a couple of birds for us,' said Steve, slyly.

'What?' said Kevin, aghast.

'That's right. Julie and Michelle, two girls from 4DG. Michelle quite fancies you.' Steve was in fact boxing clever on his own behalf as for some time he had wanted to ask Julie out but hadn't had the courage until the idea of a double date with Kevin and Michelle occurred to him. Despite his teasing of Kevin, Steve didn't have many friends at school and Kevin was at least someone who wouldn't make fun of him.

'But I hardly know her,' protested Kevin, 'and you've gone and arranged for me to spend a whole evening with her.'

'Relax. It'll be all right. You're not going out with her, just meeting her at the disco. If you don't like her you can always go home again. But you might even enjoy it.'

Steve was gradually winning Kevin around to his way of thinking. Kevin had not thought much of girls before, but the thought that he might be liked or admired by someone of the opposite sex had definite attractions and flattered his ego. He gradually succumbed to Steve's arrangements and even began to look forward to it. He was a little surprised, therefore, at the rebuff he got when he tried to interest Ginger in the idea.

'Sorry, Kevin, but it's not really my scene. Anyway it's YPF on Fridays. Aren't you coming to that?'

'Well, I would normally of course,' said Kevin, 'but this disco sounds fun, and it won't do any harm to miss YPF just once, will it?'

'No, I guess not,' said Ginger, in a voice that sounded as if he was disappointed in Kevin. 'Well, I hope you have a good time, then. See you at the weekend?'

'Yes, of course,' said Kevin, and walked away to his next lesson. He felt put out at Ginger's negative reactions and the way he'd managed to make him feel guilty. There was nothing wrong with discos after all, Ginger had had to admit that, and Kevin was determined to enjoy this one, with or without Ginger.

Friday evening saw Kevin checking his appearance carefully in front of his bedroom mirror. He had used the deodorant liberally and even 'borrowed' some of his dad's aftershave, though he hadn't started shaving yet. Now he was just putting the finishing touches with his comb and hoping that he'd captured the right image for himself with the clothes he'd chosen – trendy enough to be accepted as a disco-goer, but not so way out that he'd stand out. He'd told his parents where he was going and they'd raised no objection beyond that of setting a time limit of 11 pm, so at 7.50 he took his leave of Mum and Dad, who exchanged knowing winks and smiles, and set off for his rendezvous.

Steve was already outside the disco when he arrived and they stood waiting nervously until Julie and Michelle arrived. Kevin was quite taken with Michelle, who wore a stunning outfit and he entered the disco in high spirits. The boys paid the entrance money and they bought some shandies and found seats at the far end of the hall. Most people were doing the same as the place was still half empty and nobody had yet braved the dance floor. Kevin sat and watched the hypnotic light patterns that the strobe was making on the ceiling. There were myriads of light fragments chasing each other around the darkened room, and together with the flashing spotlights and pulsing sound from the DJ's booth, Kevin found his senses reeling with the sensation of it all.

'Sorry. What was that?' he said to the pretty brunette beside him.

'I said, "Do you want to dance now?" The floor's filling up and that's what we came here for,' said Michelle, the slightest suggestion of a pout on her lips.

'Yes, if you like,' said Kevin, and stood up with the other three, while inwardly he trembled at the thought of having to reveal his lack of dancing technique. They joined a fairly large group of dancers and Kevin found that it wasn't as difficult as he'd imagined to move in time with the music, and that most of the others were little better than him, anyway.

The evening progressed smoothly enough for Kevin, though he found it difficult to keep up a prolonged conversation with Michelle. Her interests were mainly pop stars and TV, while his were fishing, cycling and table tennis, and of course, church, but he did not dare mention that for fear of being laughed at. Still, Steve and Julie were hitting it off enthusiastically and the powerful atmosphere was having an influence on him.

It was about half past ten and a very relaxed Kevin was about to pluck up courage to ask to see Michelle home, when he noticed a slight disturbance by the door. A group of lads had just made their entrance and were jostling through the crowds to the bar. At first Kevin didn't recognise them in the dim lighting, but then the familiar leather jacket of the leader made his stomach turn over and his throat suddenly dry. The last people he wanted to meet here were Gavin, Terry, Tone and the rest of them. But maybe they wouldn't see him among the crowds in the dark room. He fervently hoped so.

Any hopes the management might have had that the newcomers would behave themselves were soon dashed when the gang, led by Gavin, decided to take to the dance floor. They barged into the dancing groups, making exaggerated movements and generally disrupting the atmosphere. Gavin, in particular, seemed to be behaving in a peculiarly hyper-active manner, and Kevin could only turn his back in cringing fear of the embarrassment of meeting him. He turned to Michelle.

'Shall we go now? I'll take you home if you like.'

'That's a bit sudden, isn't it? It's still early,' protested Michelle, clearly enjoying herself still.

'I think there's going to be trouble,' admitted Kevin. 'See those louts behind us?'

'Oh, I see what you mean. All right, then. You lead the way. I hate any kind of violence,' said Michelle as she noticed the increasingly anti-social behaviour of Gav's gang.

Unfortunately for Kevin, to leave the hall they had to squeeze past the dancers right behind Gavin, who had to choose just that moment to swing round and collide almost face-on with the boy he most despised.

'What's this I see before me?' he yelled in mocking derision. 'It's Chuck, at a disco, and all dressed up. I don't believe it!' and he let out yells of laughter, summoning the rest of the gang to look.

'Why aren't you dancing then, Chuckweed?' he called, making exaggerated gestures at Kevin that resembled a matador with a bull. Kevin made a final abortive attempt to extricate Michelle and himself from the situation.

'Leave us alone, Daley,' he muttered as he tried to push past the bully. But that was all the excuse Gavin needed.

'Who do you think you're pushing, weed?' he shouted, and shoved Kevin back hard. Then with no warning at all he waded into Kevin, fists flailing. His punches were wild and uncontrolled and other people around suffered the force of his fury. Kevin tried to protect himself as well as he could but it was a minute or two before officials were able to grapple with Gavin and finally frog-march him towards the manager's office.

Kevin found himself propelled kindly but firmly towards the exit, with Michelle following in a subdued manner. He was already feeling the effect of Gavin's fists and knew he'd have several bruises in the morning. He was winded too, and was grateful for the helping hand that steered him through the crowd towards the fresh air. Finally they were outside and he was able to take in gulps of cool night air.

'Are you all right, mate?' said a voice he recognised, and turning he looked into the face of Tone.

'Tone! I didn't realise it was you. Thanks!' said a very surprised Kevin.

'Yeh! Well never mind about that. You'd better clear off while you can. The police have been called and you don't wanna get mixed up in that, you being in the fight an' all. Take her with you and get home before there's any more trouble. Now' op it!'

Without another word, Tone retraced his steps into the hall leaving a bewildered Kevin to walk stiffly home with Michelle, as the unmistakable sound of the police siren in the distance grew gradually louder.

# 7

# A surprise visit

Kevin awoke very gingerly the next morning, feeling the effects of last night's escapade every time he turned over. His torso seemed one mass of bruises which sent a continual message of protest to his tortured brain. For his brain was preoccupied with other problems too. As he went over the events of last night in his mind he could not avoid the inescapable conclusion that he owed more to Tone than he at first realised. If Tone had not escorted him out of the hall as swiftly as he did Kevin would inevitably have been caught up in all the questions and accusations involved in the post-mortem of the fight.

Not that Kevin felt any remorse for what happened; he had tried his best to avoid Gavin, but circumstances and Gavin's belligerence had defeated him. Nevertheless, even being part of a fight at the local hall was a thought enough to bring out tiny beads of sweat on Kevin's brow. An interview by the police, having to face Gavin again, being escorted home by the police, the questions and recriminations from his parents, was too much of a nightmare to even contemplate. Yes, he had a lot to thank Tone for.

Now, as he slowly prepared himself for the day ahead he was enormously relieved that his parents knew little of last night and need know nothing more than he had told them. He had had a nice time, yes, he had remembered to escort Michelle home, and sorry he was five minutes late arriving home. That was the extent of his parents' inquiry and interest and Kevin hoped it would stay that way. Fortunately he noticed as he looked into the bathroom mirror that his face did not betray any signs of bruises like the rest of him did, so he was safe from curiosity on that score too.

He started on his usual Saturday morning chores, taking his time over the tidying and cleaning of his room – a task new to him since his mother stopped doing it when she started a part-time job at the local corner shop, and a task that he'd resented at first until he saw his mother's tired face one evening and decided that bedroom tidying was not so difficult, after all. He was still glad when it was finished, though, and he could begin on the much pleasanter chore of caring for Rusty and buying his food for the week.

The next hour saw him wandering round the supermarket searching for the best bargains. It was a shock, therefore, and an embarrassment almost to bump into the person he had so recently been thinking about.

'Hello, Tone! I didn't expect to see you here.'

'No, me neither,' mumbled Tone. The surprise was obviously mutual and for once, Tone showed faint signs of embarrassment.

'I'm buying food for my new dog,' laughed Kevin, also embarrassed, and showed Tone the contents of his basket.

Tone didn't reciprocate, though his trolley showed signs of more serious shopping.

'Got home all right last night, then?' he said, changing the subject.

'Yes, thanks. You certainly saved me from a lot of aggro.' Kevin hoped he sounded genuinely grateful.

'That's OK then,' rejoined Tone. 'We'd better get on. We're blocking up the passage.'

Kevin sensed that Tone didn't want to talk much but chance threw them together again at the checkout, where Kevin, having bought his dog food, noticed Tone struggling to pack his purchases and pay the till girl at the same time. Kevin hesitated. Should he obey his instinct to help or should he mind his own business and let Tone manage on his own as he seemed to want? Just then, Tone dropped a bag of sugar which split open, spilling its contents on to the floor. Kevin dashed over, his mind made up for him.

'Here, let me help you,' he offered to a flustered Tone.

'It's all right, I can manage,' growled Tone.

'But you'll never get all that lot into one box. Put some of it in mine,' persisted Kevin.

Tone reluctantly had to admit that Kevin was right and allowed him to share the groceries between their two boxes. So together they emerged into the busy street.

'Thanks,' said Tone, recognising Kevin's good turn. 'If you take out your stuff from the box I'll manage from here.'

'Don't be daft,' began Kevin, then stopped as he saw Tone's face darken. 'I mean, look, no offence, but wouldn't it be much easier if I carried this box for you. I don't mind, honestly, and you'll never make it trying to carry two boxes.'

Tone had to agree with Kevin's good sense so they set off down the road, Tone slightly in the lead, uneasy at the idea of being associated with the boy he had spent so long hating. After a while they left the busy main streets and Tone relaxed a little, freed somewhat from the fear of being seen with Kevin. He began to talk.

'You were lucky last night. Gavin was all set to murder you, could have done too if he hadn't had one too many.'

'You mean he was drunk?' said Kevin. 'I wondered why he was acting so strangely. He's not usually the one to lose his temper like that.'

'That's only the half of it,' went on Tone. 'Look, Chuck, don't breathe a word of this 'cos Gav's still me mate, but what 'e did last night was too much. If he'd just been drunk, he could still have pulverised you, but he'd taken some speed as well.'

'What are you talking about?' asked Kevin, bewildered.

'Where 'ave you been?' Tone exclaimed. 'Haven't you heard of speed? – amphetamines? – drugs!' he continued, as each word brought yet more astonishment to Kevin's face. 'He bought one of them brown folded-up papers from a friend – cost 'im six quid 'an all – then he slipped it in 'is drink. By the time we got to the disco he was high on it – acted like 'e wanted to run a four-minute mile. There was no stopping 'im inside – dancing like a madman. If you 'adn't copped it, someone else would've. Heaven 'elp 'im if the fuzz suspect what he was on – possession of drugs is heavy stuff. Gav's a stupid berk; I'd 'ave told 'im so an' all but he would only have 'it me too.'

Kevin was too horrified at what he heard to interrupt Tone, though there were plenty of questions he'd love to have asked. Again he was relieved that his part in last night's scene had gone undetected. If drugs had been found or even mentioned, with him involved, then his shame and disgrace would have been total. Tone had been his saviour in more ways than one, or rather, and Kevin smiled to himself, God had been looking after him last night. Despite his foolishness in going somewhere where Kevin now realised he didn't really fit, God had made sure he came to no real harm, and had used Tone to do it! 'Thanks, Lord!' Kevin murmured.

By this time they had reached Tone's house. Kevin would have handed the groceries over at the gate but Tone had obviously become used to Kevin's company.

'You may as well come in now you're here,' he said and Kevin meekly followed him around to the back door and into the kitchen. 'I guess I owe you one too for finding my dad a job,' Tone continued as they unloaded the groceries on to the table.

'What do you mean?' said Kevin.

'Your dad fixed my old man up with a job round where 'e works. It's not much, only labouring, but it's a bit better than the dole and it gets 'im out of the house.

Your dad phoned up last week. Didn't 'e tell you?'

'No, he didn't,' said Kevin. 'Tell the truth, I'd forgotten about it myself.'

'It was you, though, put 'im up to it, wasn't it?' accused Tone. 'Can't think why you bothered, but thanks anyway.'

'I reckoned I owed you something,' answered Kevin, 'after the way I treated you before. And also' – Kevin gulped as he summoned the courage to deliver the next few words – 'God told me to do it to make up for all the bad feeling there was between us.'

He'd said it now and waited for the scorn and derision that was bound to come. Strangely, it didn't happen.

'I dunno about God and all that, but if it's done our family a good turn it can't be bad,' said Tone matter of factly.

At that moment the kitchen door opened and a middle-aged woman walked in. She was wearing an orange housecoat tied crookedly over her nightdress, her feet in tattered mules, her hair unkempt and her face definitely the worse for wear. She was holding a freshly-lit cigarette and seemed to have trouble focusing on Tone and Kevin.

'Hello, Tone. Wondered where you were. What's all this lot?' she said, in a tone of confused uncertainty.

'It's the shopping, Mum,' said Tone. 'We needed some as the cupboard's low and you asked me to get it yesterday. Don't you remember?'

'Remember? Yes, of course I remember,' said Mrs. Fowler, then broke off. 'Who's this?'

'This is Kevin,' said Tone. 'He's just going.'

'Oh, don't go!' insisted Mrs. Fowler. 'You must stay and have a cup of coffee. Any friend of Tone's is welcome here, though he hardly ever brings any.'

'Mum. It doesn't matter. Kevin's gotta go,' he pleaded.

'He can have a cup of coffee first, can't he?' she

insisted and went to fill the kettle. 'Sit down, Kevin love. Coffee's coming right up.'

Kevin was too embarrassed to know what to do, but as Mrs. Fowler didn't look as though she would take any argument he sat down. Tone shrugged his shoulders and gave up the point. Mrs. Fowler proceeded to make three cups of coffee while the two boys sat in uncomfortable silence. She added milk to two cups, then thinking that she was unobserved she added to her own cup a generous measure of gin from a bottle beside the fridge. Tone noticed, saw that Kevin had too, blushed and hung his head.

Mrs. Fowler sat down at the table with them to drink her coffee. After her initial talkativeness, she subsided into a morose silence, concentrating on her drink and cigarette and oblivious of the boys' presence. Tone could stand the tension no longer and busied himself instead with putting away the groceries.

Kevin sat sipping his coffee and after a while Mrs. Fowler got up, stubbed her cigarette in the sink, and took the rest of her drink away with her, calling over her shoulder as she went, 'Nice to see you, Kevin.'

When she had left, there was another embarrassed silence which Kevin felt obliged to break.

'I guess I'd better be going.'

'You might as well stay and finish your coffee now she's made it. You've seen everything now anyway; there's no more dirty family linen to wash in public. If you hadn't insisted on carrying those groceries, it would never have 'appened,' said Tone unkindly.

'Well, look, I'm sorry, I was only trying to help. I certainly didn't mean to pry,' protested Kevin.

'Save your sympathy, Chuck,' snarled Tone, then in a placatory tone, 'you can come and 'elp me with these spuds.'

Kevin joined him at the sink where Tone had already started peeling the potatoes for lunch. For some minutes they worked together without speaking, Kevin wondering at this new side of Tone he was seeing. The hard lad of Gav's gang, who showed no feeling or favour to anyone, was here shopping and preparing vegetables for his ailing mother.

'Look,' continued Kevin, 'you don't have to worry about me blabbing to people at school. I can keep my mouth shut.'

'You'd better an' all,' warned Tone. 'Even Gav don't know about this, so I'll know who to blame if it does get around.' He hesitated, then continued, feeling he had to say something by way of explanation. 'Me old woman's not always this bad. It's just that first me dad being out of work got her down, and then she got a taste for the booze. Last night she was celebrating me old man's new job.'

'So you have to do the housework,' offered Kevin.

'Like heck! I don't do this all the time, you know. It's just that sometimes she can cope and sometimes she can't. Me old man and me brother are next to useless so it's down to me to give an 'and or nothing'd get done,' Tone pointed out belligerently.

'All right. Keep your hair on,' Kevin said placatingly.

'Yeh, well! Just so long's you get the picture. I ain't no mother's boy! Anyway you'd better 'op it now – she'll be down again in a minute.'

'Yes, OK,' said Kevin. 'See you on Monday.'

'Right,' said Tone, then added, a little sheepishly, 'and thanks for the 'elp.'

Kevin waved his goodbye and set off for home, with plenty to think about regarding the completely new Tone he'd been seeing in the past twenty-four hours.

# 8

## Winners and losers

'Hey, Tone. Do you fancy seeing a video at lunchtime?' The time was Tuesday breaktime, the enquirer Kevin Chuck. He had seen Tone standing by himself for once in the corridor and decided to take the bull by the horns.

'Wadda you mean, a video? You showing porno films or summink, Chuck?' he joked.

'No,' laughed Kevin. 'The CU is showing a film of a drama group called "Riding Lights". They've produced a video of their ten best sketches and we're going to see one of them today. We saw a couple last week and they were good – rather funny too.' Kevin rushed through his prepared speech before Tone could interrupt and pour scorn on his invitation.

'I don't like religious things; you should know that, Chuck. But I don't mind watchin' a video if it's good. I'll see,' he said, grudgingly. 'Anyway, I must be off – I'm losing valuable lighting-up time.' So saying, he trudged off to the familiar smoking ground behind the bike sheds.

So Kevin's offer was not completely rejected and he waited to see what lunch-time would bring. He had had much to think about since last Saturday and he realised he had been guilty of dismissing Tone as a no-gooder and grouping him along with all the rest of the vandals and bullies. Saturday had changed all that when he saw a totally different side to Tone's personality, and it was not without hope that he looked out for Tone's arrival in Mr. Jenkins' classroom that lunchtime.

A steady drizzle of rain had started an hour earlier, turning the playground into a water assault course. Many were glad of an excuse to go indoors, and as the video had been well publicised, a number of casual onlookers had drifted into the meeting. But Kevin still felt a thrill of excited disbelief and apprehension when Tone sauntered in with a crowd of other fourth years.

The video, called "Life is but a melancholy flower" was just beginning and the audience, though talkative during the introduction, were reasonably quiet and appreciative during the actual drama. There were one or two witticisms about a pansy dressed up as a daffodil, but generally it was well received. Mr. Jenkins started a discussion afterwards on what people thought of heaven and eternal life, but had an indifferent response from the mixture of cynical or apathetic onlookers.

Kevin sought out Tone afterwards in the lunch queue.

'What did you think of it then?' he asked expectantly.

'Not bad, I suppose,' grunted Tone. 'Very funny, that geyser dressed up as a flower. But all that rubbish about life after death and going to heaven – that left me cold!'

'I don't think it's rubbish,' said Kevin. 'I believe I'm going to heaven.'

'Maybe you are, mate, for all I know,' replied Tone. 'Maybe you come from a nice 'ome and 'ave nice parents. I don't, and I can't stand some bloke telling me I'm going to hell because I'm not a snob like him.'

'But that's not what it said!' protested Kevin. 'Mr. Jenkins told us that eternal life was for anyone who wanted it. A Christian is not a do-gooder or a millionaire,' he continued, warming to his subject, 'but just someone who wants Jesus Christ to forgive him. I had to admit I was wrong last year for the things I'd done and I had to say sorry to God and start living his way instead. That's why I'm a Christian.' Kevin hadn't meant to say so much, and now reddened as he realised others were listening besides Tone.

'Ooh! You naughty boy!' mocked Tone. 'Doing naughty things and 'aving to say sorry.' Tone realised they had an audience and made the most of it. 'You can't be a very good Christian if you've done all them bad things, so what makes you think you're any better than me? Just 'cos you've said sorry and had your sins forgiven you think that gives you the right to preach to the rest of us and tell us we're going to hell. Well you can stuff it, Chuck!' ended Tone with a derisive scorn aimed as much at his audience as at Kevin.

Kevin was devastated at this vindictive reply and turned away in embarrassment. He avoided the gaze of several pairs of eyes and queued for his lunch in silence. He wanted only to crawl away into a corner and hide from mocking or curious eyes. He had tried to speak to Tone about being a Christian, had tried to share his faith with him, and had been met with a vicious rebuff. Just when he thought that Tone was becoming interested by turning up to the meeting, and that he could even begin a friendship of sorts with Tone, it had collapsed around him like a pack of cards. It had all been a complete disaster.

Tone, meanwhile, was showing off with other fourth years around him, some of whom had also seen the video. It was easier to laugh and smirk at something which made you slightly uncomfortable and their lunchtime was spent in making fun of 'The God Squad'. Once Tone glimpsed Kevin sitting by himself on the other side of the room and felt a twinge of guilt at the way he had spurned Kevin's trusting sincerity and treated him once more like a personal enemy. But this feeling soon passed as yet another filmgoer joked about religious videos.

Kevin had almost finished his lunch when Ginger and Darren arrived at his table with their sandwiches.

'Sorry, we're late, Kevin,' said Darren. 'We stopped to help Mr. Jenkins put the equipment away. Great video, wasn't it?'

'Yeah!' agreed Ginger, 'and super to see so many extra

people there. I counted thirty-nine in all.'

'Huh! Fat lot of good it did them,' remarked Kevin sourly.

'Why? What's the matter?' asked Ginger.

Kevin nodded in Tone's direction. 'Look at 'em. Making fun of us and our Christianity! I tried to talk to Fowler afterwards and he just shouted at me to stop preaching at him. If anything it's made him worse.'

Kevin's outburst stilled the conversation and Ginger and Darren munched their sandwiches while Kevin finished his apple crumble. Eventually Darren volunteered, 'I shouldn't take all their laughing at face value, Kevin. We all know that video was good and had a message, and it probably spoke more to them than they'll ever admit.'

'But why do they have to make fun of us all the time?'

'I dunno, Kevin. But you mustn't let it get you down. We know what we believe and none of their mocking is going to change that. We'll just have to put a brave face on it. After all, people laughed at Jesus, too.' Darren's statement seemed to end the discussion and reassured Kevin. At least he had friends who wouldn't back down on their beliefs.

Shaken as he was about sharing his beliefs, and even about what he actually did believe, Kevin clung on to the friendship of his mates through the rest of the week. Friday night couldn't come quickly enough when he could forget school, Tone and his mockers and look forward to an enjoyable evening of table tennis and snooker at YPF.

He challenged Darren to a game of table tennis as soon as he arrived, and before long they were locked in the now-familiar battle of skills at the table. Kevin was even able to win one game out of three that they played, and they relaxed afterwards with a Coke, each in mutual congratulation.

'You're really coming on, Kevin,' enthused Darren.

'You'll be beating me before long.'

'Thanks for the compliment,' replied Kevin, 'but I don't think I'm that good yet.'

'But you've got a real talent for the game, Kevin,' persisted Darren, 'especially considering you only started playing a few months ago. You ought to take it more seriously.'

'I used to think I was no good at anything,' admitted Kevin. 'But perhaps you're right. I ought to practise more.'

'That reminds me. Where were you last week? I was very short of worthy opponents,' laughed Darren.

'Oh! Yes! I went down to the disco in town,' Kevin blushed at the memory.

'Oh! Was it good?'

'It was all right, I suppose,' said Kevin non-committally, while inwardly his mind was racing. Suddenly he realised where he preferred to be, where his true friends were, and that was not at the disco. His thoughts were interrupted.

'Any of you two want to play doubles?' called out a voice. It was Derek, his cheerful face beaming down at them. 'These three lads want one more,' he explained, 'and I'm so good I'd spoil their game!' That was typical Derek, always laughing and joking, but so different from Tone and his cronies. Derek always made you feel good inside, encouraged Kevin and sort of built him up.

'You play, Kevin,' Darren encouraged him. 'You exhausted me with that last game,' he joked.

'All right, if you're such an old man!' laughed Kevin, and stood up to join Derek. Only then did he notice who his opponents were, or rather, who one of them was, for standing there with a rather disgusted look on his face was Terry Boxall. He obviously would have preferred anyone but Kevin to play and looked away with deliberate disdain.

A diminutive, fresh-faced lad called Nicholas broke

into Kevin's confusion. 'You're playing with me, Kevin, against John and Terry. OK?' he prattled, unaware of the new tenseness in the atmosphere.

The game was played with little spoken between the four lads, watched nonchalantly by Darren and rather more keenly by Derek, who knew of the antagonism between Terry and Kevin and was hoping the table tennis would begin to break down the barriers. Terry began by ignoring Kevin but as he and John began to better their opponents he allowed himself an occasional superior grin when yet another smash flew past Kevin's bat.

Kevin meanwhile was suffering a mixture of emotions. Terry's supercilious smirks were not lost on him and increasingly irritated him, the more so as they were completely unfounded. John was the stronger player and made most of the winning shots, while on the other side of the table, Kevin was constantly being let down by the haphazard style of his partner, obviously a beginner. Not that Kevin minded that so much, but it was galling to have Terry, by his grins and gestures, turn it into a personal duel. At the same time he didn't want to give Terry the satisfaction of seeing him get angry and neither did he want to let a table tennis game upset him. Somewhere at the back of his mind, too, Kevin felt he was being tested. Was he going to give way to his temper and go back to the old ways of hatred and revenge which Gav's gang lived by? Terry would like that, even if he was no longer in the gang. Or was he going to lose graciously and show that he had no hard feelings towards Terry and the gang, even if they spurned and ill-treated him and made fun of the one thing he was good at – table tennis? He didn't have long to decide as the game was rapidly drawing to a close.

'Game to us,' crowed Terry, as yet another of Nicholas's returns dropped into the net. 'Hard luck, Chuck, you're obviously not up to our standard,' he continued, with the same derogatory smirk on his face.

Kevin smiled back, genuinely. 'Sorry we didn't give you a closer game,' he heard himself saying, 'but thanks, anyway. It was fun.' He turned to Nicholas. 'Thanks, Nicky. Perhaps we can play again some time. I could give you a few tips, if you like.'

'Yes, thanks,' said Nicholas. 'I'd like that.' The two walked back to where Darren and Derek were sitting, leaving Terry nonplussed and slightly open-jawed.

'Well done, Kevin,' was Derek's greeting as he sat down.

'Oh, but we lost. Didn't you see?' replied Kevin.

'Yes, I did, but I wasn't talking about the table tennis,' said Derek meaningfully, and Kevin then knew that he had won a victory far more real and lasting than anything that could be done with a ping-pong ball.

Just at that moment they were both startled by the sudden appearance at the door of a white-faced Mrs. Webb, searching the room for Ginger, who was absorbed in a game of snooker. Derek assessed the situation quickly, hurried towards Mrs. Webb, then summoned Ginger away from the game. A few minutes' conversation ensued, while Ginger fetched his coat, then mother and son departed, a drawn, tense look on Mrs. Webb's face.

Derek did not take long to enlighten them. 'Ginger's grandmother has died,' he said simply.

# 9

# An invitation

Kevin didn't feel like staying late at YPF that night so he left promptly at ten o'clock. The atmosphere in the room had become subdued as the news of Ginger's bereavement passed around. He and Darren spent some time discussing it, feeling sorry for Ginger but realising that there was nothing they could do about it. Others had expressed sympathy too and it had dampened the high spirits of nearly everyone. As Kevin walked home he felt for his friend. The one who had been a friend in need so often to Kevin, now stood in need of a friend himself. Kevin determined to do what he could to support Ginger in this crisis. 'Lord, be with him and let him know that you are close. Oh, and please show me what I can do to help,' he prayed.

Kevin's prayer was answered much sooner than he expected. There were more lights on than usual at home, and as he opened the back door, he sensed there were visitors in the house. In the hallway he spotted a small suitcase and sitting together on the living room sofa were Ginger and his mother. Mr. Chuck was trying to engage them in small talk while Kevin's mother could he heard moving things around upstairs. Mr. Chuck looked quite relieved to see his son.

'Oh, hello, Kevin. I expect you're surprised to see Andy here, but you see. . . .'

'Yes, Dad, I know,' interrupted Kevin quietly. 'We were told at YPF.' He looked at Ginger and his mother. 'I'm sorry,' was all he could think of to say.

'Thank you, Kevin,' said Mrs. Webb, 'but as I was explaining to your father, it wasn't totally unexpected. I guessed when I went to see her last time that she was very frail, and it was only a matter of time. . . .' her voice trailed away, lost in sadness and memory.

'Yes, well, as I said,' continued an embarrassed Mr. Chuck. 'Andy is very welcome to stay here again as long as he needs to. Doreen's turning Kevin's bedroom round now for him.'

'Thank you so much, Mr. Chuck, – sorry, Alan,' she said, forcing a smile. 'It should only be for a few days while all the arrangements are made and the funeral takes place. There's no one else to do it, you see. But it is very good of you. I don't know what I would have done without your kindness.'

'Don't mention it.' Mr. Chuck's mind turned with relief to more practical matters. 'What time is your train?'

'Six thirty, tomorrow morning. There are several people I shall have to see and some of them only work Saturday morning, so it will mean an early start,' explained Mrs. Webb.

'Yes it will,' came a voice from the doorway as Mrs. Chuck rejoined them from making up Ginger's bed. 'So we mustn't keep you talking. You must go home and get what sleep you can. Though I don't suppose you feel like much.' Kevin noticed with surprise the almost sisterly concern in his mother's voice. 'Alan will run you home, won't you, dear?'

So after a few more parting words with Ginger, Mrs. Webb left with Mr. Chuck. Mrs. Chuck gave both boys hot drinks and shooed them off to bed, fussing over Ginger like a mother hen. It was her way of showing she cared, Kevin realised, and smiled to himself.

Neither of them could sleep, though, and Kevin tried desperately to keep the conversation going without mentioning the one subject they were both thinking about. In the end, Ginger could take no more.

'It's all right, Kev. You don't have to go on, but I

78

appreciate it. I don't mind talking about it.'

'Well, what was she like then?' asked Kevin, relieved that Ginger had wanted to talk about it.

'I didn't really meet her that many times – only in the last years since Grandad died and she was left on her own. But then it was always such a long way to go, and Mum found it difficult to get time off work.'

'But why did your mum move so far away, especially if she was on her own?'

'She wasn't on her own to begin with. She came to London with my dad. You see,' explained Ginger, 'my grandparents didn't want her to marry my dad. There was a row about it and Mum went off and got married in a hurry. I don't know what the row was all about – Mum wouldn't tell me all the details – but I know that what she did upset Gran and Grandad. They weren't even invited to the wedding and it hurt them dreadfully. Then later on, of course, when I was small my dad left Mum. Mum felt awful. She'd turned her back on her parents to marry my dad, then when he left, she was all on her own.'

'Why didn't she go back home then?' asked Kevin.

'Dunno really. Pride, I suppose, or maybe she thought they wouldn't want to have anything to do with her. But I think too she felt guilty for what she'd done and couldn't bring herself to face them. I think she thought they'd never be able to forgive her.'

'But were your grandparents Christians?'

'Oh yes, and so was Mum. I don't think Dad was, though. That was the funny thing. All three of them were Christians, but none of them could say sorry or get themselves together again. Anyway, then Grandad died about five years ago, and that did the trick. Mum and Gran got together again and they got quite close. Mum thought of moving up there but she didn't think it would work, all three of us living together, and then she didn't think she'd get a job up there, either. But they were always phoning each other up or writing, and we used to go up there every holiday and Christmas. It was sad, really.'

'Sad!?' exclaimed Kevin. 'That sounds like it ended really well.'

'Yes, no, what I mean is,' Ginger explained haltingly, 'they were close the last few years, but what about all the other years? What if Mum had said sorry years ago, when Grandad was still alive, what would have happened then? If Gran was so ready to forgive and make up five years ago, why couldn't she and Grandad have done the same ten years ago?'

There was silence in the bedroom for a while and Ginger began to think that Kevin had fallen asleep. But Kevin was thinking.

'I suppose it's rather like us,' he said at last.

'What do you mean?' said Ginger.

'Well, we're often slow to say sorry to God, either because we're too proud or too ashamed to own up and ask forgiveness. But all the time God wants to forgive us and be friends again. All we do is hurt ourselves and God and stay miserable, all because we don't say sorry quick enough.'

'You're right, Kevin. I never thought of it like that,' said Ginger, and drifted off into a dreamless sleep.

Kevin and Ginger enjoyed their weekend together, more than either of them thought they would. As neither of them felt very energetic, Kevin and Rusty took Ginger to the local river on Saturday and introduced him to the gentle sport of fishing. It was completely new to Ginger and he was intrigued by the varied collection of hooks, weights and bait that Kevin had accumulated. He tried his hand at casting and became even more fascinated than Kevin in watching for every ripple of water or movement of the line. When tea-time came they had caught nothing but had spent an absorbing afternoon far away from sombre thoughts of death and funerals. The whole weekend was a tonic for Ginger, and Kevin found his prayers for his friend answered. Without realising it, he became just the companion that Ginger needed. They both looked forward to the new week with hope and confidence.

Maybe it was Kevin's air of extra cheerfulness and friendliness that week that prompted Tone to speak to him, or maybe it was a slight sense of guilt for his harsh words of the previous week. But whatever it was, Tone approached Kevin in a conciliatory way.

'Hey, Chuck, how's things?'

Kevin masked his surprise and replied nonchalantly. 'OK, thanks, how about you?'

'Not too bad. Would be a lot better if I weren't in this dump. The weekends are the only thing worth livin' for – so long as me mum's not drunk an' I don't have to 'ang around the 'ouse too much.' He paused. 'Saw you on Saturday, down by the river, fishing with yer mate, what's 'is name?'

'You mean Ginger?' offered Kevin.

'Yeh, that's right. Fishing's no good for me – too slow. Catch anything?'

'No,' admitted Kevin. 'Not our lucky day.'

'Too bad. I like fish, mind you, when I can eat 'em. I do my fishing down the local chippy,' joked Tone. 'It beats school dinners any day.'

'You could be right there,' agreed Kevin. 'There's nothing I like on the menu on Wednesdays.'

'Well why do you put up with it? You can always come down the chippy with us if you like. You can get a pass from old Fletcher at breaktime. You gotta leave school sharp on twelve though, 'cos there's always a queue.'

The bell for first lesson ended any further conversation and they parted, Kevin pondering on the fact that he had just more or less accepted a lunch invitation, and from a most unlikely source. He was quietly pleased at this sudden turn of events and although he was cautious of Tone's moods, which seemed as changeable as the weather, he looked forward once more to a better relationship with Tone, and to a change of scenery at twelve o'clock.

With a busy morning of maths and English, and getting his lunch pass at breaktime, Kevin saw nothing of Ginger or Darren, so it was in a somewhat apprehensive mood that he made his way out of the school gates to the fish and chip shop a quarter of a mile down the road. He saw no sign of Tone so wondered if he'd find himself foolishly eating fish and chips on his own. But sure enough, when he arrived, he found Tone in the queue ahead of him, along with Alan and Paul, two other members of Gav's gang. Kevin looked around for Gav and Terry but he remembered that they weren't so regular in their school attendance this year, which probably accounted for their absence. Alan and Paul looked rather sneeringly at Kevin but Tone acknowledged his presence and obviously persuaded the others to wait for him, for when Kevin emerged with his cod and chips they were standing outside.

Nothing was said while they enjoyed the taste of their salt and vinegar-laden lunch and soon other Woodenders joined them with the same appetising food. When the last splinters of batter were eaten and screwed up papers kicked or thrown away, the group mooched off. Too early yet to return to school, too cold to stand still, they combed the streets, looking vainly for warmth and shelter.

Kevin wandered with them, uncertain of his purpose yet not wanting to appear wet or anti-social. It was Tone who seemed to know where he was going, and led them to a street where disused warehouses dominated shops and houses, which squatted in between like untidy dominoes.

'Come on,' called Tone. 'I know a way into this one,' and he expertly mounted a window sill to prise away two loose boards. The others followed, some with more enthusiasm than others, while a few, including Kevin, hung back through fear, before deciding that warmth and togetherness was preferable to the cold November wind.

Inside was musty and smelly, but out of the wind and dry. It took Kevin a while to get his eyes accustomed to the semi-darkness and the first thing that he noticed was that most of the others had passed the cigarettes around and were lighting up. Someone even offered Kevin one which he politely declined, but he leant against the wall wishing he'd never come and becoming more and more aware of his embarrassing position. Conversation was limited to a few corny jokes and rude comments, and Kevin knew no-one except Tone whom he could at least talk to. Why did he have to get himself into such awkward situations? It was like the disco all over again. Still, Tone had saved him from that one and Kevin was trying to show Tone the same friendship. It was that fact alone which held Kevin there, though his mental agony increased by the minute. 'Lord, help me!' he pleaded silently.

It was his watch that saved him, or rather the time. Glancing down at his wrist, Kevin suddenly realised that afternoon school was only ten minutes away, and that they'd better leave if they weren't going to be late.

'Hey, Tone!' he called. 'It's five to one. We'd better go.'

'What's your hurry, Chuck?' Tone replied with deliberate bravado. 'There's plenty of time. Sit down and relax.'

'I don't think we ought to. We'll be late if we don't go now.' A slightly pleading note had entered Kevin's voice.

'Why bother? It's warmer here. We was thinking of

bunking school anyway, eh lads?' Other lads cheered and laughed at Tone's suggestion as his impudence gave them courage. Kevin found himself isolated.

'Well, I'm sorry. I'm going back,' he said flatly, and climbed back through the window to the street. Two or three others followed him accompanied by a chorus of cat calls and jeers from inside the warehouse. It was a thoughtful and depressed Kevin who returned to school that afternoon, wondering if he'd done any good at all in the last hour. Apart from the fish and chips it had all been rather boring and a waste of time. If that was Tone's way of life he could keep it. But that thought gave Kevin no satisfaction as he ploughed his way through the long afternoon of French and geography.

# 10

# A matter of life and death

Kevin heaved a huge sigh of relief as he filed out of the geography room with the rest of the class, eager to escape to the liberty of the streets and home. Wednesday afternoon was far from Kevin's favourite and his embarrassing lunchtime experience only deepened the gloom that settled over a dismal and boring afternoon. He sauntered out of the school's main door, turning his collar up at the drizzly atmosphere. Not the weather to lift your spirits but anything was better than the stuffy, overheated classroom he had just left. Taking a deep breath he joined the noisy throng jogging and jostling through the school gates.

Just then he noticed a figure hurrying in the opposite direction to everyone else. His initial mild surprise turned to astonishment as he recognised Tone's gangly figure, but a very different Tone from the one he had left two hours before. White-faced and breathless, this was not at all the confident and swaggering ringleader most people knew. Kevin was immediately concerned. Instinctively he hailed the distracted figure.

'Tone! Over here!' he called as Tone looked round, bewildered. He ran straight to Kevin, breathless and distraught. 'What on earth's the matter? You look awful,' said Kevin, shocked at the sight before him.

'Quick!' gasped Tone. 'Yer gotta help me, Kev. Gotta phone – ambulance.' All this interspersed with great gulps of air.

'Why? What's happened?' frowned Kevin. 'Of course I'll help, but tell me. What's gone wrong?'

'It's Whelan, in the warehouse – 'e fell – 'it 'is

'ead – 'e's dead!'

'What!' Kevin was rooted to the spot.

'Come on! We gotta phone!' panted Tone, and he almost dragged Kevin across the road to the nearest phone box, narrowly missing two hooting cars in the process. Kevin was nonplussed at this drastic turn of events and his mind whirled to try to catch up with what Tone had just said.

'How do you know he's dead, Tone?' he said at last. 'People don't usually die just from a bang on the head.'

Tone reluctantly slowed his pace. ' 'e's not breathing!' he spat out fiercely. 'And 'e's ever so still. We even felt 'is pulse. Nothin'! Come on!' he pleaded as Kevin still dragged his feet. 'You gotta phone!'

At the phone box, Kevin picked up the receiver. Tone was obviously in no fit state to speak controllably. He dialled 999.

'Emergency. Which service?' said a detached voice at the other end.

'Er. Ambulance, please.' Kevin waited while the connection was made. 'Could you send an ambulance to – er –' Kevin looked at Tone, who whispered 'Albermarle Street.'

'Hang on, son,' said a calm male voice at the other end. 'What's your name and who's been hurt?'

'I'm Kevin Chuck and the boy hurt is John Whelan. He's lying in one of the warehouses. He fell over and banged his head.'

'How do you know all this, son? Were you there?' came the voice.

'No, but a friend of mine was,' said Kevin.

'Oh yes?' said the now-suspicious man. 'And what's his name?'

'Keep me out of this!' hissed Tone in Kevin's ear.

'Er – he's just a friend of mine,' said Kevin lamely. 'Look, are you going to send the ambulance or not?'

'Yes, all right, son. Albermarle Street, you said?' The

man obviously suspected a hoax and Kevin thankfully at last put the receiver down.

'Right. That's done! They're sending one straight away,' Kevin informed Tone. 'We'll have to hurry if we're going to get there in time.'

'I'm not going back there. I can't face it!' wailed Tone. 'How can you even think of it?'

'But we might be able to help,' explained Kevin. Fear of seeing a dead body had never occurred to him. 'Besides, you've gotta face up to it, Tone. You were in the warehouse. You ought to be there now.'

Tone said nothing and it was Kevin now who dictated the pace and firmly led Tone to retrace his steps to the warehouse. There was little time for explanation but Kevin gathered that the Whelan boy had fallen backwards against an exposed steel pillar and immediately crashed to the floor. 'Broke 'is neck,' was Tone's grim conviction.

Albermarle Street presented its usual air of peaceful decay when they arrived, with no ambulance yet to shatter the unsuspecting calm. Outside the warehouse they paused.

'I ain't going back in there!' Tone was slightly hysterical at the thought of reliving his real-life nightmare.

'All right. Stay out there and wait for the ambulance. I'll see what I can do.' And with a cool decisiveness which amazed him when he later recalled the events, Kevin vaulted up and over the window sill.

When his eyes were once more accustomed to the half light, he saw immediately the limp form of John Whelan slumped in a lifeless heap among the rubble. Bending over him, Kevin could detect no breathing and no pulse from his wrist. He fought against the rising tide of panic and puzzled furiously for something to do. For the second time in that place he cried out to God, 'What am I going to do?'

Suddenly, pictures flashed across his mind of another similar situation, of him and Ginger standing beside a road, miles from anywhere, him panicking and Ginger quietly praying. Then that amazing, miraculous ride home. Well, God gave one almighty answer to prayer that day, but this! This was too much to ask, wasn't it? And besides, the ambulance would arrive soon and it would be too late then – probably was already. Yet the memories kept coming and seemed to encourage him to go ahead.

Slowly he knelt beside the body as the words of prayer came to him, rising in him and flooding through and out of him in an endless stream of words. What he said or how long he knelt there he could not afterwards say, but the next thing he remembered was the sound of the two ambulancemen stumbling and cursing over the rubble-strewn floor.

'Now then, young man, let's have a look,' said the first one, laying a hand on Kevin's shoulder. Kevin moved aside to let him examine the body. The ambulanceman did his job expertly and quickly, but the seconds of silence were too much for Kevin's taut nerves.

'He is dead, isn't he?' he blurted out at last.

The man finished feeling John's wrist. 'No, son, he's not. He's been knocked unconscious, good and proper, and he'll have an almighty headache when he wakes up, but he'll be all right.'

'But he wasn't breathing!' Kevin protested. 'And I felt his pulse – there was nothing!'

'You were probably feeling his wrist in the wrong place – it's easily done, especially when the pulse is weak, like it is. Don't you worry, son. He'll be as right as rain as soon as we get him to hospital. What's his name, and address?'

'John Whelan, but I don't know his address. He goes to Wood End School, though.'

'All right. Leave it to us. He's in good hands now.

You better go out and tell your friend the good news. He looked as white as a sheet when we arrived.'

Kevin forced a smile and obeyed, giving only a backward glance at the ambulancemen gently lifting John on to the stretcher. He re-emerged into the daylight of Albermarle Street in a happy daze to break the news to Tone.

But Tone was nowhere to be seen. A small crowd had gathered by now but Kevin searched the faces in vain. He avoided the curious, questioning glances and waited only for the ambulance to depart before setting off himself for home. He was bursting to tell Tone the good news but there was so much to think about. What had happened back there in the warehouse? Had John Whelan really been dead? The ambulanceman said not, and he should know. Probably both Kevin and Tone had simply failed to find the pulse. And yet? And yet? Kevin could not work it all out. But one thing he did know. He had prayed, and God had answered. His heart leapt at the exciting realisation of the power of prayer.

'Oi, Kevin! Over here!' Kevin's thoughts jerked back to the present.

'Tone! Where did you get to?'

'I couldn't hang around there. All those people staring. I cleared off before they started to ask questions or called the police.'

'There'll be no need for police, Tone. John's alive!'

'Stop kidding me! He was as stiff as a post when I left 'im!'

'It's true, Tone! The ambulanceman found his pulse and said he was just unconscious. They've taken him off to hospital.'

Tone let out a long sigh of relief. 'Thank God for that!'

'You never spoke a truer word, Tone. You see, when I saw John lying there, back in the warehouse, I had this sudden urge to – well – to pray for him.' Kevin felt a bit sheepish but carried on. 'It seemed the best thing to do, and it looks as if it worked.'

'You mean, God answered your prayer!' Tone finished it for him. 'Stroll on! There's more to you than meets the eye, Chuck!'

Kevin smiled. 'I don't think it had a lot to do with me. Like you said, "Thank God for it". By the way, do you think you could drop the Chuck bit?'

Tone laughed. 'Yeh, all right, Kev,' and playfully punched Kevin on the arm. 'Well that's it, I suppose. See ya tomorrow!'

'Hang on,' objected Kevin. 'Shouldn't we tell someone? Where does he live?'

'Cooper Street, but you can forget that. I'm not going round there.'

'Oh, come on, Tone. I know it was an accident but you were there. You ought to tell.' Tone said nothing, finding something in the gutter that needed his undivided attention. 'It was an accident, I take it?' persisted Kevin. 'Tone?'

Tone gave the merest shake of the head. 'We 'ad an argument. I said he owed me a fag and he wouldn't give me one – said it was his last. We started fighting, then I kicked 'im where it hurts. He doubled up,' – Tone paused, unwilling to verbalise the final admission of guilt – 'then I punched him in the face – that's when he fell.'

There was silence. Kevin didn't know what to say and they walked without speaking until their homeward routes diverged and they parted with the briefest farewell. Kevin was shocked and Tone knew it. Tone was a rough diamond and a bully at times, but Kevin knew the other side of Tone, the Tone who did the shopping, even the housework for his inadequate mother, who cared for someone he could easily have despised. There was the Tone too, who even when they were enemies had made overtures of friendship to Kevin, had even got him out of that nasty situation at the disco. All of this made Tone's cowardly and spiteful attack on John Whelan the more shocking. Kevin walked home numb.

Tone meanwhile was experiencing real shame for the first time in his life. He'd done some devious, thuggish, even illegal things before – some he'd smirked at, some he'd not been so proud of. But this one act with its almost fatal consequences fell on his spirit like the final doom. There was no excuse and he knew it. Tone hated himself and his life. He didn't blame Kevin for hating him either.

But Kevin didn't hate him. He had to talk it all through and as soon as tea was over, couldn't wait to bike round to Ginger's and tell him the momentous news. It took a long time and Ginger was just as excited at the tremendous answer to Kevin's prayer and just as concerned at the plight of John Whelan as Kevin himself was.

'But what should I do about Tone?' asked Kevin. 'He did a terrible thing to poor John, and I didn't know what to say to him.'

'I expect he knows what he did wrong,' said Ginger. 'But what he doesn't know is how you're going to treat him now, you know.'

'I see. You mean, am I going to turn my back on him or still be friends?'

'Or act smug and superior because you're a religious goody-goody,' Ginger goaded him.

'But I wouldn't do that!' protested Kevin.

'Well it's up to you – up to us – to show him that, isn't it?' said Ginger.

'Yes, I see what you mean,' mused Kevin, as he tried to think of ways he could show Tone that he still cared, to cement their now-shaky friendship. He grinned suddenly. 'I wonder if he plays table tennis.'

# 11

## Snooker, bikes and Jesus

'Good shot, Terry mate. Just pocket the blue and we're there.' Friday night at the YPF was in full swing and the snooker table was attracting its usual share of interest. Kevin turned his attention from the table tennis to watch Terry clinch the game with a flourish and turn to grin at his partner. Terry and Tone, the terrible two, they had jokingly become known in the ten weeks since Tone started coming. Kevin smiled at the satisfying thought that Tone was now an established member of YPF, partly through his friendship with Terry but partly through Kevin's influence too.

Mind you, Tone had reacted cautiously at first to Kevin, afraid of his disapproval and rejection. The whole school soon got to know what had happened at the warehouse and either cold-shouldered him or idolised him. But only Kevin had got behind the mask and seen the terrified, guilt-ridden, lonely teenager. It would have been easy for Kevin to feel smug and superior.

But that hadn't happened. Kevin and Ginger had shown a real friendship very different from the hate or fear that everybody else showed. They hadn't been ashamed to be seen with Tone, a fact that baffled him, and out of school had even seemed to like his company.

That first Saturday had been a hoot. The three of them fumbled round the supermarket doing Mrs. Fowler's shopping, making hilarious efforts to control their rogue shopping trolley. Then the afternoon saw Kevin's vain attempt to get the others 'hooked' on fishing. Tone couldn't stand the stillness and quiet, even though he was the only one who landed anything sizeable. It had been a laugh, though, and Tone had promised to show them some real action when he next went to a bike trials meet.

Tone was unsure about the invitation to YPF, but when he met Terry there, decided it wasn't so bad after all. After a few weeks he even had to admit that the 'religious lot' weren't quite such freaks after all, and as for Derek, he and Tone seemed to share the same sense of humour and were always bantering with one another.

Then there was the fateful day when John Whelan returned to school, fully recovered but with no love lost between him and Tone. Poor Tone! All his hangers-on expected him to stage a showdown with Whelan and continually egged him on, while all Tone wanted to do was run away and hide. He couldn't face meeting John and was tormented by the reminder of his own guilt. That was the day he had asked Kevin for Derek's address and had gone round there for a chat. He hadn't said much about that, but Derek had had a quiet word with Kevin and Ginger and told them to pray hard for Tone.

From then on, Tone gradually changed. He seemed almost visibly to take on a new air of confidence without any of his former smug cynicism. His admirers soon dropped away but he hadn't cared. He seemed to relish his odd-ball friendship with Kevin and Ginger, and had even been seen in church with them, causing a few raised eyebrows at the leather gear he wore. He never missed a YPF meeting now, though he preferred to stick to snooker rather than be thrashed by Kevin at table tennis.

'Did ya see that then, Kev?' called out Tone. 'The terrible two strike again. It's a good job I joined this club so me and Terry could show you all how to play snooker!' And he laughed at his own joke, as did the others at the brash but likeable newcomer in their midst. He left the table and joined Kevin over a can of Coke.

'All set for tomorrow, then, Kev?' he asked. 'It's the first big meet of the year. You'll enjoy it.'

'Yeh. You bet,' replied Kevin. 'You'll have to explain the rules to me, though. I don't know the first thing about trial biking.'

'Dead simple, mate. I'll give you all the low-down on the way. Me bruvver's driving us.'

'Does he mind me coming?' said Kevin.

'Nah, 'e's all right, so long as I keep on the right side of him.' A sudden thought struck him. 'You'd better stay off the religious bit, though, Kev. You know, don't mention God an' that. Me bruvver hates all that stuff. He's a right heathen.'

'What does he think of you coming to YPF then?' asked Kevin, slightly amused.

'Well, 'e doesn't know – at least, not that it's in a church. I just tell 'im it's a youth club I'm going to.'

'What about your parents?'

Tone's face darkened. 'Fat lot they care. Dad spends all his time in front of the telly, and Mum –' he paused – 'well, you know about Mum, don't you?'

'Yes, of course,' said Kevin sympathetically. 'Is she any better?'

'On and off,' sighed Tone ruefully. 'She's not too bad so long as nobody upsets her. We all try to keep on the right side of her. But it's not easy.'

'It must be murder,' agreed Kevin. 'I don't know how you put up with it.'

'It's bin better lately,' said Tone, 'ever since I had that chat with Derek. He 'elped me a lot, talking about God wanting to forgive me and Jesus being able to sort out the mess I'm in. It's made me start to feel sorry for Mum and not get so angry.' He paused. ' 'cos I know I need sorting out too, like over Whelan. Had to say sorry to God for that, didn't I? Feel a whole lot better since.'

'But you still swear and get angry,' Kevin pointed out tactlessly. 'I heard your language when you missed that pot in snooker.'

'All right, smart alec,' fumed Tone. 'What yer gonna

do about it?' he threatened.

'Nothing,' said Kevin, seeing the danger signs and wanting to placate Tone as soon as possible.

'Good.' Tone smiled grimly. 'I thought for a moment you didn't wanna come to the meet, after all.'

Kevin saw the twinkle in Tone's eye and knew it was all right.

'There is one thing I can do about it,' he said with a wide grin.

'Oh yeah? What's that?'

'Pray about it for you. Derek said you'd need a lot of prayer.'

'Dead right there too. Yeah, you do that, Kev mate, I could use it. I need to do some of that praying meself.' Tone looked round. 'Hey, look sharp, the table's free. Come on. Give you a game – that is, if you don't mind being thrashed!'

Kevin laughed and for once allowed Tone to have the last word.